Tumbleweeds

Chasing Dreams, Desires, and Destiny Across the Texas Oil Patch

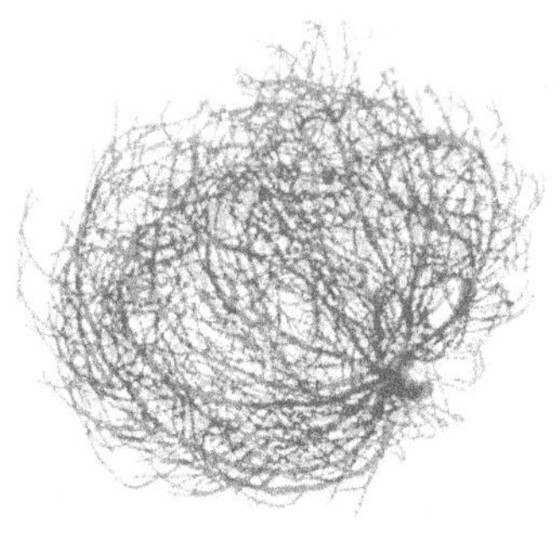

Benny Richards

PROLOGUE

THE VAST OILFIELDS of Texas between Abilene and Fort Stockton are referred to by many as "The Big Country." The towns, big and small, that dot the landscape there are all unique in their own way. However, as different as they may be, they all share two things in common…oil and cattle. Along with the cattle comes the horse culture. Long ago the Comanche ruled those open plains where only the strongest survived. Then came the cowboys who tamed the area for later generations. Cowboys still work and ride the mesquite covered hills to this day. The next to arrive were strong, hard, young men from everywhere seeking to make their fortunes in the oil patch. Some were successful, while others were left financially and physically broken. Generations of farmers, ranchers, oilmen and their families call West Texas home.

The wind-blown hills of the Big Country can be desert-hot in the summer or bitter cold in the winter. The harsh unforgiving landscape there creates tough people who are tied closely to the land. People who work hard, play hard, and love hard.

This is the story about two such people who meet by sheer chance on a late Sunday afternoon at truck stop in a small town. That unexpected meeting would turn into a whirlwind romance with life-long consequences for both of them and also everyone around them.

The story begins on April 19th, 2015

CHAPTER 1

The last Sunday of each month was very stressful on Rolly. Two years ago a judge in Nolan County granted him visitation with his son on the second and fourth weekend of each month. Ever since then, he had been meeting his ex-wife halfway in Colorado City to hand off their kid like a football. Every time he had to watch little Jake get in that car and drive away, it ripped at his guts, but there wasn't anything he could do. His hands had been tied by a court. Things weren't so bad when he was staying just down the street from his young son and ex-wife in Sweetwater. Back then, he got to go to most of the tee ball games and would get glimpses of Jake around town. But being flat broke had caused Rolly to sell all his tools and head to the oil field like so many others.

This Sunday afternoon was a particularly bad one. When they met at the post office parking lot, Donna started her shit as usual. And par for the course, she used Jake as a bargaining chip. It seemed to her the child support payments he was making right on time each month were not quite enough for her and she wanted more. An argument ensued. Now all he wanted to do was get back to his trailer. The previous week had been long and hard and the one coming up looked to be just as tough. He just needed to get back to the trailer and sleep off some frustration.

Headed west, he was on I-20 in the left passing lane attempting to pass a long line of 18-wheelers in the right lane. That's when something caught his eye in the rear-view mirror. A white car in his lane was hauling ass and coming up on him quickly…very quickly. He glanced down at his speedometer. 75 mph was what it told him. He thought, "Damn, they must be going 90 or more." He would have moved over and gotten out of the way but the big rigs on the right and the Range Rover in front of him had him blocked right where he was at. Then the white car was on his back bumper swerving back and forth, weaving side to side, and flashing headlights. The female driver who he could clearly see now in the mirror, wanted him out of her way. Rolly assumed there must be some sort of emergency, but he could do nothing. A closer examination of his rear-view mirror began to tell a different story. The two females in the car appeared to be laughing. What the hell? In another quarter mile a small gap opened up just ahead of a semi in the right lane. As soon as he was clear he jerked the wheel to the right and moved over. Now the white car, a Dodge Challenger, moved up and took his place behind the Range Rover. A little pissed by now Rolly looked over, trying to figure out what the damn hurry was. That's when he locked eyes with a blonde headed woman in the passenger seat. She was smiling at him and giving no indication of any emergency that would require riding his bumper. Then, suddenly the road opened up in front of the Challenger and off they went. As the car quickly pulled away, the blonde looked back, winked, and blew him a kiss. Rolly, no longer pissed, just smiled back and waved. That woman, whoever she was, had just made his day. He watched as the Challenger disappeared in the distance with long blonde hair blowing in the wind outside the passenger window.

Just before the exit for Coahoma he remembered he needed fuel and that he had not eaten. Choices around the little town were limited, at best. He decided to head on down to Big Spring and get gas and grub. When he took exit 179 there was an old Hank Williams song playing on the radio. Pulling into the parking lot of the big truck stop on the edge of town he noticed pump number 8 was open down at the end. He hopped out and used his credit card to purchase 50 bucks worth of diesel. After placing the pump in the tank, he tilted his hat back on his head and leaned up against the bed of the truck. He was doing some people watching and checking out the other vehicles when he saw it. Well, well, well…a certain white Dodge Challenger was two rows over parked at the pumps. Guess who was still riding shotgun in the passenger seat. Blondie! She had his full attention now because of their brief encounter a few minutes earlier back on the interstate highway. The pump kicked off and he was replacing the fuel cap when it happened. A sight that would be seared into his memory. The passenger door of the Challenger swung open and out stepped Blondie. Wow! His world stopped spinning for a brief few seconds as he stood and stared. She had both hands full of empty glass bottles as she walked toward the trash can. Adult beverages no doubt. After depositing the empties in the can she turned and headed back to the car.

She didn't just walk…she strutted. The sleeveless party dress she was wearing hugged her slender body tightly in all the right places. The sequins on the dress glittered like a million diamonds in the late afternoon sun. Never before had he seen such a sight in dusty West Texas. Rolly had thrown off all his bashfulness around women a long time ago. That was good because he was determined to meet this woman. Trying to come up with the right witty one-liner, he wondered if she was as flirty in person as she was at a distance riding down the highway. He had just a few seconds to make up his mind. Finally, he thought, "To hell with it, why not?" He decided to introduce himself to this mystery woman. As he approached the car, Blondie looked up and saw him coming. To discourage any interaction she looked off in the opposite direction. Now standing beside the open passenger window Rolly said, "Hello." She turned to him and replied simply, "Hey." And this is how it went from there.

"You two girls all right?"

"What two girls? I'm the only one here."

"Yeah, but you have a lead-footed friend around here somewhere."

"Do I know you?'

"Well, I thought y'all were going to run me in the ditch a few minutes ago back there on the highway."

"Oh, was that you? Awful sorry about that. That's a nice hat…are you a cowboy?"

"Maybe, but I don't own any cows. Hey, tell me your name."

"I'm Lucy…my name is Lucy."

Rolly knew she was lying, and there was no damn way in hell she was giving up her name to a total stranger standing in a parking lot at a truck stop. Leaning on the car now with both hands on the door, he continued.

"You don't look like a Lucy to me. What do your friends call you?"

"Why, Cowboy? Do you want to be my friend?"

He would have been pissed off at her sarcasm if he wasn't so paralyzed by her good looks. Before he could say another word a loud female voice from just over his shoulder, began berating his ass. Her name was Tonya, the owner of the Challenger. She was a little tipsy and a little obnoxious.

"Get away from my car! Are you fucking homeless or something?"

Then Blondie looked up at Rolly and said, "Oops…time for you to leave."

Tonya continued her verbal assault, "Damn panhandlers, go find a life!"

Blondie told her friend, "Tonya just shut up and get in, it's ok."

Turning back to Rolly, who was standing speechless, Blondie said, "See ya."

Getting behind the wheel Tonya added, "Yeah, but I wouldn't wanna be ya."

As the car sped out of the parking lot, a last empty bottle was thrown from the driver's window into the ditch as the Challenger turned onto the highway.

Rolly just stood there disgusted with himself. He had been shot down. She had him on the ropes from the very first word spoken and he knew it. He just mumbled to himself, "Well, I screwed that up." Walking back to his truck, he figured that would be the last time he would ever see the mystery woman again. Racing up the ramp to the interstate, Tonya asked Blondie, "Who the hell was that? Did you know that guy?"

"That's the guy you almost ass-ended earlier."

"Really? What the hell? Did he follow us to town?"

"No, he was just getting gas."

"What was he saying? What did he want?"

"He wanted my name and probably my phone number."

"Please tell me you didn't give it to him."

"No but I should have. He was kinda fine."

"Oh my God, you are such a whore."

"Ha! That's pretty rich…a tramp like you gonna call me a whore."

The two best friends just laughed and headed home.

CHAPTER 2

EARLY MAY IN the Texas oil fields is warm and windy. The well site prep gig that Rolly just landed wasn't what he wanted to do for the rest of his life, but it paid well for the time being. The crew he worked with were tasked with getting areas ready for oil rigs. They built roads, laid water lines, prepared mud pits, and dug pilot holes. Basically, they did everything needed to get ready for actual drilling to get started. Rolly got to use the construction skills he had learned from his grandfather. Some days he was a welder. Some days he drove a skid steer to clear brush and level ground. Other days he poured concrete, erected fence, moved dirt, or just did cleanup work. The six-man crew he worked with was a rough bunch and he was the best among them. He was tough. Losing his parents at such an early age and then being raised by his grandparents was hard on him and his older brother. He never got to enjoy the finer things in life when he was young, but he learned the value of hard work and gained a sense of pride. Two traits that would serve him well later in life.

A dirty dusty month dragged by slowly. Rolly never missed a day. He was never a minute late for work either. It wasn't long before his hard work and dedication caught the attention of his boss, Hoss Spurling. Hoss began his career in the oil patch over four decades earlier. He started out as a worm, moved up to tool pusher, and eventually became drilling superintendent. Hoss was now the wealthy owner of the Thunder River Ranch and founder of the Spurling Energy Company. The energy company was his meal ticket. The ranch was his hobby. Hoss was a no-nonsense man and knew a valuable employee when he saw one. He quickly took a liking to Rolly. In early June Hoss promoted Rolly to foreman over all three of the well site prep crews working under Spurling Energy Company contracts. This was great news for Rolly! A pay raise meant he could keep up with his increasing child support. The company truck and fuel card he was given took the place of putting gas in his own pickup truck.

The days and weeks rolled by and Rolly enjoyed his new position. Hoss was happy because whenever a problem came up, he knew he had a man on site that could handle it and get things moving again. All the crew members were satisfied because they answered to a man who practiced common sense and was firm but fair. For the first time in a long time, things were looking up for Rolly.

One Friday morning, Rolly and his #3 crew were finishing up a job ahead of schedule just before lunch. The second time these guys had done so in a month. Rolly was so pleased with them he decided to treat them to a meal in Big Spring. Upon arriving at Maria's Mexican Cantina, the crew all sat down at a large table near the front door. Menus in hand, they all began to mull over their picks and order, one by one. Rolly decided to try out the chicken quesadillas. After handing the menus back to the waitress he relaxed and took a good look around the place. The dining room was packed with lots of people. He smiled and waved at a couple of familiar faces in the back. Then he noticed the gentleman seated at the next table was wearing some sort of uniform. It turned out to be an airline pilot's flight uniform. He then noticed a very attractive woman wearing scrubs sitting beside the gentleman. It was hard to tell just how attractive she really was because her blonde hair was pulled back into a bun and her face was buried in her cell phone. But then several moments later she looked up from her phone. Unbelievable…Rolly did a double take just to make sure. It was Blondie. Rolly immediately pulled up a memory. He never forgot a face, especially this one. He then thought to himself, "I'll be damned, so she is married to a pilot." He then wondered if Mr.Pilot knew what a wild child he was married to and if he knew his woman wore that huge diamond ring selectively. He tried to recall their previous conversation at the truck stop and thought, "Lucy, my ass…she ain't no Lucy." Then she happened to look straight at him. Rolly never hesitated. He winked at her and blew her a kiss just as she had done to him two months before. Her expression showed surprise at first but then…but oh then he could see she recognized him too. She glanced to her right at her husband to see if he was aware of any of this. He was too busy nursing his frozen margarita. She then turned her head back to Rolly. With her jaw clenched and her eyes squinted in an evil fashion, she gave him the most go to hell look like, "Don't you even think about it." He was quite entertained at this point. Paybacks are hell and it was payback time. Checking her out now from head to toe, he noticed she was wearing a small name badge. Jess was all it said. Now he had a name. A five-minute staring contest went on between Rolly and her before the pilot and his wife began to pay out and leave. As the couple walked by the crew's table headed for the front door, she took one last quick look. Rolly was waiting. He blew her another kiss and sarcastically rolled his fingers up and down to say goodbye. One of the crew members saw this and warned, "Look out, vato, that guy will kick your ass for fucking with his old lady." He just laughed and said, "Nah." Those quesadillas tasted better than ever for some reason that day. Jess was pissed after walking out of the cantina. The nerve of that oil field trash, pulling that in front of her husband. What if Curtis would have seen him? Damn him! She got in the car and slammed the door. On the way home she started thinking about that afternoon back at the truck stop where she first encountered Rolly. She replayed everything, at least the parts she could remember. She finally came to the conclusion, hell maybe I deserved that back there. Random thoughts kept rolling through her mind, and a few questions kept popping up. What if Curtis would have realized what was going on back there? What if that guy had made a scene? How would Curtis have reacted? She was fairly certain how he would have reacted twenty years ago. But what about now? She wondered. She had been wondering about a lot of things lately. The relationship between Jess and her husband was still good by most people's standards, but Jess' standards were not most people's.

Jess and Curtis met in college at a frat party. She was a pledge in one of the sororities, and one of the sisters introduced them. He was a junior in the ROTC program, majoring in engineering and freshman women. She was a recent graduate of Riverside High School in Stephenville. Curtis graduated as valedictorian of his high school class. Jess was no valedictorian, but she was a two-time homecoming queen. He was the son of a general in the Air Force. She was the daughter of former State Senator Hatch McBride. Getting accepted to the big university in Fort Worth was not difficult for either of them. Money and influence talks. They had a whirlwind romance the first two semesters she was on campus.

The fun and games slowed down considerably the third semester when she came up pregnant. Plans changed overnight for her, but not so much for him. Oh, he did what seemed like the right thing to do at the time. He married her. Appearances must be maintained in some families. It was six years before she would get back into school, then four more before she would realize her dream of becoming a nurse. Curtis went on to follow in his father's footsteps and became a pilot. He eventually landed a spot in the cockpit flying commercial airliners out of Lubbock. In the 21 years since they met, Jess and Curtis had been on a roller coaster ride of a marriage. There were ups and downs, especially during the six years he was serving in the Air Force, while she was taking night classes and working full-time waiting tables. The birth of their daughter Nikki was the glue that held them together in the beginning. Jess had been an honest and trustworthy wife. There was that little thing with that police officer, but there was no sex involved so she didn't count that. Curtis, being a pilot, was always flying all over the country for days at a time. And of course, he was a guy so who knows what secrets he was hiding. In more recent years, Jess and Curtis had settled into a routine. A very boring and unfulfilling one from her perspective. She did the nurse thing four days a week. She cooked and cleaned when she was at home. She ran errands and kept the bills paid. She also found time for a one-hour dance class once a week. Curtis was a sure bet to be at the table on Wednesday poker night. Golf on Saturday morning when he was in town, and Sunday nights were spent with his buddies watching football at Sonny's Sports Bar.

Jess actually enjoyed him being away so much. His drinking and his hobbies kept him out of her face. Not that she didn't love her husband...she did. However, passion and intimacy had left the scene. Curtis wasn't the firm and fit Air Force cadet he once was. He was rather short, balding, with the beginning of a pot belly. Although, in his flight uniform he still looked professional. But what the hell? He helped keep her in a new car, huge house, country club membership, numerous vacations, and Nikki's tuition was paid. She didn't have anything to complain about, right? Wrong. She had wants and needs, same as any woman and they weren't being met at home. Particularly, Jess was a Tiger shark in bed, and she was interested in finding a new ocean to swim in. She wouldn't have to wait much longer to find one.

EXIT 174
BUSINESS LOOP 20
BUSINESS
Big Spring
1 MILE
H

CHAPTER 3

ROLLY WAS ON A ROLL. It seemed that everything he touched as of late turned to gold. Hoss asked him to come by the supervisor's trailer after work one afternoon and floored him with an unbelievable offer. Seemed that Hoss' Mexican that lived on and cared for the ranch had gotten in deep trouble with the law. It meant going to prison or going back south of the border in a hurry. Mexico sounded like the more comfortable choice. Hoss was in a bind now. He needed a new overseer to take care of the ranch. He trusted Rolly more than anyone he knew so the job was his if he wanted it. Hell yes, he wanted it. Now he could get out of that trailer he'd been living in.

Being the ranch foreman was simple really. Live at the guest house. Feed a few horses and cows. Take wealthy clients hunting and get them drunk. Keep trespassers away. For Rolly it was a no-brainer. The ranch was plush, even the guest house. The extra pay combined with his regular oil field check was a God-send, especially with an ex like Donna. But most of all, this meant Jake would have a real place to come to on his visits. No more sleeping and eating in a 24-foot trailer sitting in a gravel parking lot. His young son could learn to fish, learn to hunt, ride his bike, throw a ball around, and maybe get a dog. Rolly was beside himself with excitement. He moved in the next day and time seemed to fly by.

It was late summer, and the oil field was booming. Rolly stayed busy in his foreman's role. Back out at the ranch, summer heat meant moving cattle around to better grass. One Saturday morning Rolly had just returned to the ranch from a trip to the feed store, with a load of range cubes. As he pulled around the big barn he saw the cowboys having a difficult time unloading steers out of a trailer and into a metal corral. Wanting to lend a hand, he hustled over to the trailer to hold open the rear gate as the cattle were herded out. He made a stupid mistake. While trying to tie open the gate, he stuck his hand between it and the metal corral just as a 500-pound steer was coming out. The animal slammed into the gate, crushing his hand and wrist. Jerking his hand back, he took one look at the damage and knew immediately it was time to see a doctor. He wrapped his hand tightly with an old rag he found in the front seat of his truck and headed to town.

Rolly strolled into the emergency room leaving a slight blood trail behind him. The receptionist behind the glass took one look at his mangled hand and let him go immediately back to an examination room. While closing the door, the kind woman said," A nurse will be right in."

A few seconds later, just as she had promised, the door opened and in walked a nurse with a very familiar face. Shutting the door behind her, she looked up at Rolly sitting on the edge of the examining table. She stopped dead in her tracks. Their eyes locked on each other and there was a brief moment of complete silence as both gathered their thoughts. Redirecting her eyes on his injury, she walked to him and slowly began to unwrap the blood-soaked rag.

Rolly spoke first, "So, you're a nurse?"

Continuing to examine the two-inch gash in his hand, she replied smugly, "What was your first clue?"

"You don't like me, do you?"

Again, smugly she said, "I don't even know you."

Looking at her name badge Rolly asked, "Is your name Jess?"

She stopped what she was doing and looked straight at him. "Well, I guess at least you can read."

He asked, "Hey, Jess, can we just start all over?" And then it happened. A small grin formed at the corner of her mouth, which caused a similar grin on his face.

She asked, "What is your name, Cowboy?"

"My name is Rolly, ma'am. And I want you to know I'm sorry about all that stuff at the restaurant."

"Forget it we're even, and don't call me ma'am please."

"I'd like to shake your hand, but I can't."

The two just laughed. The ice was now broken. Cleaning his wound, she had a hard time reconciling his hands with his baby-face. His hands were callused and thick. His shirt sleeves hugged his biceps snugly. This was no boy; this was a well-developed man. But that face...she wondered if he could even grow a beard. His dark brown unkept hair made him look like a teenager. The doctor finally came in, took one look, and ordered x-rays. The good news was nothing was broken, but the bad cut required nine stitches. After sewing him up, the doctor advised Rolly that the nurse would be administering a tetanus injection. The doctor wished him well and left the room.

Jess came back in carrying a tray that held some painful looking utensils. Holding up a syringe she asked, "Arm or ass?"

He pleaded, "Doesn't it come in a pill?"

She laughed and said, "Bend over, Cowboy."

After finishing up business, Jess instructed Rolly to check with the receptionist for payment. He wasn't even close to being ready to leave. He felt an almost uncontrollable attraction to her. Yeah, he knew she was married but at the moment didn't care.

"Hey, Jess, can I get your phone number? I'd like to talk to you again, sometime."

She just smiled, ducked her head, held out her hand and said, "This big ole ring on my finger says that might not be such a good idea."

Accepting her denial he got up off the table and made his way toward the door. At the very last moment before disappearing into the hallway, Jess spoke up.

"Hey, Rolly, are you on Facebook?"

Even though he wasn't, he lied and said, "Yeah, I'm on it, why?"

She said, "Send me a friend request…Jessica McBride Chapman."

He closed the door and walked away.

At the front desk he asked to borrow a pen. He wrote her name across his forearm. After signing some insurance forms he jogged to his truck. Rolly now needed help setting up a Facebook account. Never before did he have time for such foolishness, now he was going to make the time. When it came to social media stuff, he didn't have a clue, but he knew someone who did. Maria, the maid at the ranch, was always on her phone. She could help and he would be grateful to her for sharing her experience. Walking through the door at the main lodge, he found Maria vacuuming floors. After explaining to her about all the bandages, he told her what he needed from her. She smiled and took his phone. They sat on the couch together for an hour as she gave him a crash course on navigating the Facebook universe. When she had finished, he attempted to stand up but she grabbed his wrist.

"Wait just a minute, you can't leave yet. Tell me about your new girlfriend."

Rolly, playing totally innocent asked, "What makes you think I have a new girlfriend?"

"Because it's written all over your face, and we women know these things."

After a couple of seconds of staring at the floor, Rolly smiled and said, "I'm not saying I do have a girlfriend and I ain't saying I don't. Just hold that thought and ask me again in a month."

Maria just busted out laughing and said something in Spanish he didn't understand. He walked out to his pickup and climbed inside. After leaning the seat back he began his search. It didn't take long and there she was. Jessica McBride Chapman from Big Spring, Texas. There it was, all right in front of him. Answers to questions he was dying to know. He studied her profile up and down, and back and forth, like a college kid cramming for a final exam. He confirmed that yes, she was married and had a daughter, too. He was stunned to find out that she was several years older than him. Looking through her pictures he was able to come up with an image of what he thought her life was like.

After taking it all in, he just sat there thinking to himself with his finger hovering over the friend request tab. He kept asking himself, "Do I really want to do this? If I do this, isn't it just going to start some crap I don't need?" He couldn't talk himself out of it. He was too smitten to turn back. Rolly punched the add button. He had no idea about the lasting consequences that friend request would have. Nursing his injured hand, he went back to work, taking care of his responsibilities in the oil field and on the ranch. He didn't let his cell phone get out of his sight for the rest of that day and the next. Waiting on a reply was agonizing. "Was she just screwing with me? Is she just laughing at me and blowing me off?" Those negative thoughts were racing around in his head. Then, three days later it happened. That silly little ping on his cell phone, letting him know he had a message.

JESSICA MCBRIDE CHAPMAN ACCEPTED YOUR FRIEND REQUEST

He couldn't get a return message typed fast enough.

"HI, Jess, I've been waiting to hear from you."

She immediately replied, "Sorry it took so long, things have been crazy at the hospital and at home."

"No problem. Hey, how about that phone number, can I get it now?"

Jess wasn't so eager. She had been pursued by lovesick men before and she knew it was time to tap the breaks. She replied, "Whoa, Cowboy…we just got to be friends. I've got to run now, talk again soon." Seeing her hesitation to carry things any further he didn't push the issue. He ended the conversation with one last message.

"Ok cool. It was good to hear from you. Please don't be a stranger."

They traded emoji's and that was it, at least for a while.

The two new Facebook friends settled back into their routines. For Jess' part she kept her mind off her less than exciting marriage by spending time with Nikki, who was home on summer break from her college studies down in San Angelo. The mother-daughter team passed the rest of the summer shopping, dining out, and laying out in the sun by the pool. Tonya made an appearance occasionally which gave the trio an opportunity to gossip about Nikki's love life. Rolly poured himself into his work and there was lots of it. The American economy was roaring. The Spurling energy company was growing and things at the ranch kept humming along, too.

The hot Texas summer began to wind down. In late August, after Nikki returned to college for the Fall semester, Jess and Curtis left town to go on a cruise that he had booked months in advance. Leaving Galveston, they would sail the Caribbean for seven days and six nights. Jess was really excited because this was just her kind of thing. She longed for the excitement. She loved the nightlife. She imagined fine dining, dancing, and adventurous excursions ashore. Her bags were filled with new clothes and her new sexy swimwear. The scene was all set, but it would not end the way she had envisioned it. There would be trouble on the high seas.

CHAPTER 4

THE SHIP LEFT GALVESTON just after noon. By late afternoon, Jess and Curtis had unpacked and stored their things in their first-class room on the upper deck. The first stop afterward was at the pool to have some fun in the sun. Later, the couple enjoyed a gourmet meal and ended the first day listening to live music. Things were going great at this point.

After breakfast the next morning, there were lots of options for things to do. Curtis suggested trying their luck at the Blackjack table in the casino downstairs. Jess, wanting to be agreeable, tagged along. Once seated at the table, Curtis ordered his first drink and the gambling began. He had a streak of good luck right away. This just fueled his taste for another drink…and then another. One hour turned into two. The casino filled up with tourists and the crowd began to get a little annoying. Finally, Jess had had enough Blackjack. When she asked Curtis to wrap it up, he insisted on a few more hands. She wasn't having any of it.

"I've got a better idea."

"What's that?"

"You stay here and play your cards. I'm going to look around in the shops. I'll be back later."

Without waiting for a response, she got up and walked away. Curtis was now gambling big time with more than just cards. He just didn't seem to realize it, or maybe just didn't care. She took her time in the dress shops and was not bashful when using her credit card to purchase make-up, perfume, and other necessary items on her list. She even scheduled an appointment for later that afternoon at the spa to get a massage and pedicure. At a small bistro she enjoyed a veggie wrap while doing some people watching. When she returned to the casino Curtis was gone. She had a good idea where she would find him. When she entered the cabin, there he was, passed out lying in the center of the bed. She made no attempt to wake him. She just decided to let him sleep it off. After gathering a few things, she quietly closed the door behind her.

The rest of that day and the next Curtis and Jess were together, but not really. There was not much conversation. They were just going through the motions. By the fourth morning she was feeling guilty. They had planned this cruise over a year in advance as a way to spend more time together. She began to have thoughts that maybe she was being bitchy and decided to try to make the best of the time they had left on the ship. There was a six-hour shore stop in Cancun scheduled for that day. She rolled over and laid her head on his chest and asked, "What do you want to do today on shore?"

"I don't know, have you made any plans?"

"Well, I found this company that does shallow water scuba diving. Does that sound like fun?"

"Yeah, that does sound cool…but can I run something by you?"

"Ok, what?"

"Glenn called me and wanted to know if we would go fishing with him and Felicia."

"Wait…wait…Called you? When did he call you?"

"Last week. He said they were going to be at their beach house down here all this week."

Jess sat straight up in bed after hearing this and after a long pause she asked, "You knew this for a week and are just now getting around to telling me?"

"We don't have to go. I'll just tell him no."

Jess didn't much care for Glenn and couldn't stand the sight of his wife Felicia either. While thinking the matter over, she remembered her previous thoughts about spending time together and salvaging the trip.

"No, Curtis, don't tell him no. It's fine, we'll go fishing."

"Are you sure?"

"Yes, I'm sure. Let's just go."

Glenn and Felicia picked them up at the pier and then drove straight to a nearby favorite bar. While laughing, Glenn explained, "It's hard to fish when you're thirsty."

Jess had heard this story before and knew how it would end. At the bar Curtis and his buddy traded pilot stories while Jess had to endure Felicia's ramblings about politics, cooking, the weather, and all things uninteresting. Finally, after getting their buzz going, the gentlemen were ready to leave the bar and fish. All the gear was loaded into the rented 26-foot Mako and the group headed out. They cruised along just within sight of land for thirty minutes before stopping at what Glenn described as his secret spot. Hooks were baited and lowered over the side of the boat. Jess continued to pretend to listen to Felicia's thoughts on the upcoming presidential election. She was really more interested in watching as her husband and his friend get shitfaced.

Felicia was in mid-sentence when Jess stood up, let out a very noticeable sigh and asked, "Hey, Glenn when you said secret spot did you mean to fish or drink?" She then grabbed a beach towel and went to the bow of the boat. There she stripped down to her bikini, laid down across the towel and began to sunbathe. The boat was mostly silent after that.

Once back on shore it was a short trip back to the pier. The two couples bid each other goodbye at the ramp. Jess and Curtis boarded the cruise ship to begin the trip back to Texas. At the halfway point the cruise was becoming a disappointment. On the fourth night of the trip they tried sex, just out of boredom. That turned out to be a disappointment, as well. From that point, without any discussion, they both realized it would be best just to get through it and get back home. That's exactly what they did. They got through with polite but meaningless conversation. They attended a couple more shows, ate well, chatted with other passengers, but both were ready for it to be over.

On the last night of the cruise the big boat was 200 miles south of New Orleans headed west. When the clock struck twelve, Jess was still wide awake. Curtis was busy sleeping off his final round of alcohol. She decided to go for a walk around the upper deck. She wrapped a towel around her waist and quietly left the cabin. After a couple of slow laps, she stopped at the pool. Even at this late hour there were several couples still swimming. She picked out a recliner poolside, sat back, and began to scroll through her cell phone. Over the next hour most of the people had left, with the exception of one young couple at the opposite end of the pool. Those two showed no signs of calling it a night. In fact, with the absence of other people, they began to become very romantic.

Without it being too obvious, Jess watched as the couple traded kisses and held each other. No doubt about what their hands were doing beneath the water's surface. She almost became jealous as she watched the intimate display. She wanted that, too. She continued to check the status of friends on social media, making a comment here and there. Then, a face popped up that she had not thought of lately. Rolly Burnett's profile picture was staring back at her. She thought about him and their last conversation. She then wondered. She then hesitated. She then sent a message.

"Hey, Cowboy, you awake?"

Back in Big Spring, Texas Rolly was sound asleep but awakened by the sound of his phone chirping on the nightstand. He sat up and grabbed his phone, thinking there must be some emergency for someone to message him so late. He couldn't believe his eyes. Jessica McBride Chapman had sent him a message. He quickly replied, "Yeah I'm awake, what's up?"

"Why are you still up?"

"I could ask you the same thing."

"LOL."

"Where are you? Is everything ok?"

"Everything is fine. I'm stuck on a ship in the middle of the Gulf of Mexico."

"No, really…where are you?"

"I really am, we're on a cruise."

"Ohhhh…is it a good time?"

"It could be if I had the right cruise partner."

"Hmmmm…is that why you messaged me?"

"Ha ha, smart ass."

"Can I ask you where your husband is right now?"

"He's asleep. I'm sitting out by the pool."

Jess and Rolly continued their first uninterrupted meaningful conversation late through the night until the early morning. Around 5:00 am Jess waved the white flag.

"I'm having trouble keeping my eyes open."

"Well, why don't you go get some sleep?"

"Yeah, I guess I should. We arrive at the port at 2:00 today."

"Yep…you definitely better get some sleep."

"What about you? When do you have to be back at work again?"

"In two hours."

"WTF? OMG! Are you serious?"

"Yeah, but no biggie."

"I'm sorry, I didn't know."

"Don't worry about it. I wouldn't have missed this talk for a million dollars."

"You are sweet."

"Sweet enough to take you to lunch this week?"

She didn't reply. She was thinking. Her mind was racing. Her brain was saying no. The woman in her was screaming yes. He asked again.

"So yes or no, can I buy your lunch, please?"

"Ok, we can do something like that. I'll message you when I get home."

"Okee Dokee…I can't wait."

"Good night."

"Nitey-nite."

Jess just sat quietly thinking about everything that had been said. Within minutes she had dozed off lying in the recliner. When the sun came up over the back of the ship, she was still sleeping. She was awakened by a crew member who stopped by to check on her. Jess gathered her belongings and went to her cabin. When she got there Curtis was awake and pissed off.

"Where the hell have you been?"

"I'm sorry I fell asleep by the pool."

"The pool?"

"Yes, Curtis, the pool. The big hole with water in it, that pool."

"Do you expect me to believe you have been sleeping at the pool all night?"

She then unloaded on him. Enough was enough and she had had enough.

"I don't give a piper's piss what you believe. Are you accusing me of something? If you would stay sober for more than an hour, maybe you could keep up with the comings and goings of your wife."

She walked back out of the cabin slamming the door behind her. Later that afternoon they boarded a plane for the two hour flight home. Not a word was spoken between the two.

CHAPTER 5

OVER THE COURSE of the next week, the couple settled back into their routine at home. Curtis resumed his flight schedule and Jess went back to her day shift at the hospital. However, there was a new distance between them. Their relationship was broken and neither of them seemed to be in a hurry or in the mood to make the needed repairs. Jess did make good on her promise to call Rolly. She had genuinely enjoyed their previous late-night conversation and wanted more. Late on a Sunday afternoon she dialed his number.

"Hey, Cowboy whatcha doin'?"

"I've been sitting here for days now staring at the phone waiting for you to call."

"You are such a liar!"

"No, really, I haven't eaten or slept in over a week."

"Oh, shut up. Are you still interested in doing lunch?"

"No, I changed my mind."

"Would you please be serious for just one second?"

"Ok…yes I would like to do lunch."

"Are you familiar with the McAlister's across the street from the hospital?"

"Yeah, I know where it is."

"Well, I'm working the day shift all this month. I get an hour lunch break. I could meet you there."

"What day?"

"Is Tuesday good for you?"

"Yeah, that'll work."

"Ok, it's a date."

"Hey by the way, how did your cruise go?"

"Ehh…I'll tell you about it later."

"Alright, I'll see you Tuesday."

"Don't be late."

"Not a chance."

After hanging up he was giddy with excitement. In particular, he liked her choice of words. She had referred to their upcoming lunch meeting at the sandwich shop as a date.

His workload on the ranch and in the oil field, and the anticipation of finally getting to spend some quality time with his new lady friend kept him busy. The next three days flew by. On that Tuesday morning, Rolly made sure to get his crews lined out early with specific instructions on where to go and what to do. He wanted no interruptions during his all-important lunch engagement planned for later. He returned to the ranch long enough to check on animals and cowboys, and then take a quick shower. He left the guest house wearing his best shirt and a pair of starched jeans. Across the way, over at the main lodge, he spotted Maria hanging a basket of flowers on the front porch. This gave him an idea. He whistled at her and gave her a wave as he loaded up for the trip to Big Spring. In town he made a short visit to a local florist, and then he was ready.

He arrived a few minutes early, so he sat in the truck checking text messages from Hoss and his work crews. That's when he got an incoming text from Jess. "Hey, I'm leaving the hospital now. I'm walking over." He looked up and saw her walk outside through the emergency room doors. After waiting for her to stroll across the manicured lawn, and then cross the street, he got out and met her in the parking lot. She greeted him with a big smile. He pulled a single long-stemmed rose from behind his back and presented it to her. Her mouth fell open and she took a look back over her shoulder toward the hospital before taking the flower.

"Well…ok then…thank you."

"Is everything ok?"

"Yes, I just didn't expect this but it's good, thank you."

They walked inside together and got in line to order their meal. The next 45 minutes could only be described as a hectic blur of small talk. They talked about the weather, pets, and politics. They discussed their jobs and their families and even what music they liked best. The one topic both avoided, however, was her marital status. The time passed too quickly for him and then it was time for her to get back to work across the street. She walked him back to his truck.

There was a brief awkward moment as both were trying to find the right words to end the lunch date. Finally, he just looked at her and said, "I wanna do this again." She was chewing on her bottom lip trying to think of how to reply.

"Hey, Rolly, listen, thank you for this rose and I enjoyed lunch, but if we are going to do this, I have some rules."

"Ok, what?"

"Let's keep everything loose. Please don't get too clingy. I have to be careful, ok?"

He just nodded his head in agreement and said, "Ok." He then held out a fist. She just laughed and responded with a fist bump.

"Is that loose enough?"

"Yeah, loose enough. I'll text ya later."

Text, she did. The next text turned into five more. Five texts turned into fifty. Fifty turned into several hundred. For the next three weeks their Tuesday lunch hours were spent at various restaurants around town. They started to get very comfortable around each other.

During that time, he was able to think over his evolving relationship with Jess. He was uncomfortable with her marital status but what was he to do? It had just been so long since his divorce. He wanted a woman in his life. He needed a woman in his life. He wanted her to be that woman. She had all the credentials he was looking for. She was gorgeous. She was educated. She had class. She had the right personality, and she was making herself available.

The only downside he had identified so far was her damn cell phone. She never let it out of her sight. Not for one second. Oh well, just a minor irritation, nothing to fret about for now. But also, what about honesty? He did think about the fact that she was doing things behind her husband's back. If her husband couldn't trust her then, should he? All these negative thoughts were getting in the way of what he wanted. He wanted her and had a plan to proceed forward. At their next lunchtime together, he put everything into motion. After finishing their meal, he asked,

"Hey, listen, if you don't already have plans for this Saturday, there's somewhere I would like to take you."

She rested her chin in the palms of her hands with her fingers cradling her face. Batting her eyelids like a child she asked, "Are you asking me out on a date?"

"I guess you could call it that. My boss has a horse running in Ruidoso and he wants me to come watch. I would really like to take you with me."

"When would we get back? Curtis will get home early Sunday."

"The races start around noon, I think. His race is at four.

If we leave at eight in the morning, we can catch most of the races and still be back by nine or ten that night."

"Let me think about it, ok?"

"Think about it hard, ok?"

She giggled, he smiled, they both got up and walked out into the parking lot. He walked her to her car and sent her off with a hug.

To his great pleasure everything fell into place. She thought about his invitation overnight and agreed to go. Curtis was going to be gone that Saturday, so she was free. Saturday morning he met her in one of the back hospital parking lots where she left her car. They stopped to grab a bite to eat for breakfast and then headed to New Mexico.

They got seated at the track just prior to the first race. It was a bright and sunny day. Rolly and Jess shared small talk as the races progressed. At one point she became interested in the large belt buckle he wore.

"Tell me about your belt buckle."

"I won it in San Angelo while I was in college there."

Leaning forward to get a better look she asked, "What does it say?"

"Well, it had my name on it and it used to say Bareback Champion San Angelo Stock Show and Rodeo. Plus, it had the date also."

"You're gonna have to win another one pretty soon. That one has some serious mileage on it."

"Yeah, it's hard to read now but if this old buckle could talk man, it could tell some stories."

She looked at him and smiled, "I have no doubt." Finally, the most important race of the day was about to begin. Hoss' horse was ready to run. As the horses paraded past the crowds seated in the grandstands, Jess asked, "Which one is his?"

"His is the one out front. He's the number one horse." He was a tall grey thoroughbred mounted by a seasoned jockey with a winning record.

"He is pretty."

"Let's just hope he is fast."

"How much did you bet on him?"

"One hundred bucks."

"Oh wow, how long is this race?"

"Six furlongs, it's basically one lap around the track."

"My gosh I don't see how they do that in this heat."

"He drew a bad position."

"Really?"

"Yeah, he's in the first lane on the railing. A lot of times, horses against the rail get squeezed off."

"You seem to know a lot about this."

"A little bit, when I was younger I thought I wanted to be a jockey."

"Why didn't you do it?"

"I didn't fit. Those Jockeys are little bitty fellas."

The horses reached the starting gate and a few seconds later they were off and running. The number one horse Tequila Sunrise, got off to a surprisingly good start. At the half-way point, he held a commanding led over the other eight horses. That was the best news of the day. After that, it was all downhill as, one by one, he was passed on the outside by the entire pack. Ole' Tequila finished dead last. Rolly and Jess looked at one another. She made a sad face and he just shook his head.

"Man, if I know Hoss, he ain't taking this too well. Let's go get something to drink, I'm dry." They made a quick trip to the restrooms and then the concession area. Then as they were returning to their seats, Rolly saw Hoss talking to a trainer while standing on the track against the grandstands. "Hey, come on, I want to introduce you to Hoss."

She followed along as they made their way down the steps then weaved through the crowd over to the edge of the track. Hoss saw them coming, which put a big smile on his face.

"Well, I see you did make it after all."

"Yep, wouldn't have missed it."

"Who is this pretty lady you have with you?"

"Hoss, this is Jess."

Hoss took off his hat and tipped his head forward as he gently shook her hand.

"Sorry you drove all this way to see my horse do so poorly."

Jess just smiled and said, "Well, some days you got it and some days you don't."

"Well today sure wasn't his day, I hope you didn't lose anything on him."

"Hoss, I'm sure next time he'll win first place."

"He better or he'll be pulling a wagon somewhere in Mexico." They all three had a big laugh. "Hey, Rolly, are y'all staying overnight? I've got dinner reservations for later at the Cattle Baron. It's my treat, come and join us."

"Naw, Hoss, I appreciate the offer but we gotta get back."

"Okay then, suit yourself but if you change your mind y'all are welcome."

Turning to Jess he then said, "And don't you be a stranger, pretty lady, it would be good to see you again." Jess gave him a big hug, then the two men shook hands and parted ways.

Rolly pointed his truck east and they left the mountain town to start the four-hour trip back home. He was content thinking his date had genuinely enjoyed her day. Not long after getting on the highway, she began to ask a lot of questions about Rolly's former wife. She seemed to be suddenly curious about the details of his first marriage, especially how it ended. It wasn't an overly complicated story actually, and he explained. He and Donna met behind the bucking chutes at a rodeo in Hobbs, New Mexico. At the time, she was a two-time champion barrel racer and hometown hero. Rolly was riding bucking horses bareback on the weekends to make a few extra bucks. They had a short whirlwind romance before she ended up pregnant. Both of them fell back on their upbringing and decided to do what they thought was the right thing. They got married.

The marriage didn't get off to a very good start. Donna got into a few scrapes with the law. First was a drunk driving charge, followed by an arrest for stealing pills from the pharmacy where she worked. The final straw for Rolly was the trail of hot checks his wife left all across West Texas. He had no intentions of being married to a thief addicted to pain medication and booze. After three short years, the marriage ended in a bitter divorce. The only thing they had to show for their troubles was little Jake.

Rolly took Jess' interest in his former love life as a good sign. Maybe she was trying to figure out where she could fit in. Maybe she was trying to learn what mistakes others before her had made so she wouldn't repeat them. He didn't know but was glad she was showing enough interest in his life to ask questions. It was getting dark when they crossed the state line.

"I'm getting sleepy."

"Why don't you take a nap?"

"I don't think I could, sitting up."

"Well, here let me move this."

He lifted the center console into an upright position, opening up the front set for her to lie down. She took his offer and curled up with her head resting on his lap. He laid his arm gently across her stomach and she responded by wrapping both her arms around his. Within minutes she was asleep. As he drove through the night along the deserted highway, he glanced down often. The soft blue light from the dashboard was just enough to illuminate her face. He studied every detail as she peacefully rested. Taken by her beauty, emotions began to stir inside him that he hadn't felt in some time. Things looked to be going his way in their new relationship. He desperately wanted this. He needed this. It had been too long since he had felt this. They arrived back at the hospital parking lot around 10:00 p.m.

CHAPTER 6

NIKKI'S UNEXPECTED CALL caught Jess totally off-guard and unprepared. Jess had snuck out of town without telling anyone. And under the current circumstances, she wasn't going to be much help to her daughter.

"Mom, I have a huge problem."

"What... what's going on, baby?"

"I've got a flat tire."

"Well, can you fix it?"

"Mom, you know I can't, I don't even know where the jack is."

"Where are you?"

"I'm in Midland."

"What are you doing in Midland?"

"I decided to come home this weekend. Melissa asked me to go to the game and watch Tony play tonight."

"Nikki, I wish you would tell me these things."

"Are you still at work?"

"No, I'm not. Actually, I'm not even in town."

"Where is Dad?"

"He won't be back until Monday."

"What am I going to do? I'm sitting on the interstate across from the big white oil tanks."

These words scared Jess. She knew that was a busy and dangerous stretch of roadway. She needed to figure something out fast, but what was she to do? Then she remembered something. It was something Rolly had told her in a text the night before. She told her daughter that she would call her right back and then dialed his number and held her breath.

"Hello."

"Hey, Rolly, it's me."

"Duh...I can hear that."

"Ha, ha that's funny. Listen, I need some help."

"Okay, name it, what do you need?"

"Are you still in Midland? Didn't you say you had to go over there this morning?"

"Yeah, I'm here. I've got to drop off a load of pipe then I'm going back."

"Oh, thank God! Can you please do me a favor? Nikki is in Midland right now with a flat tire. She's sitting across the highway from those big white storage tanks. Can you please go help her? I'm worried about her in all that traffic, those trucks don't even slow down."

"Yeah, ok, let me drop off this trailer and I'll head that way now."

"Thank you so much, Rolly. I'm going to text you her number so you can speak directly to her, ok?"

"That's fine, I'll call her right now."

"Rolly, you don't know how much I appreciate this."

"It's not a problem. Hey, where are you...at work?"

"Uhhhh...no I'm off today."

"I thought you were working Fridays now."

"Uhhhh, yeah but I traded a shift. I needed to go take care of something."

"Is everything ok?"

"Yes, everything is fine but please hurry if you can."

"Don't worry about it I'm on it."

He hung up and called Nikki who was patiently waiting.

"Hello?"

"Hey, Nikki my name is Rolly Burnett. I just talked to your mom. I'm on my way to you now."

"Do you know where I am?"

"Yes, she told me everything. I'll be there in ten minutes, just stay inside the car."

"Ok…thank you."

He arrived just before noon. When he pulled up Nikki popped out and met him at the rear of her car. After a brief introduction, he assessed the situation.

"Hmmmm…well, you're not gonna get any more use out of that tire. It's ruined."

She pointed west back down the interstate and told him, "It happened back there, but there wasn't a good place to pull over. These trucks scare me." She was wise to have a healthy fear of the big rigs roaring by at 75 mph only feet away.

"Open your trunk, we're gonna need the spare tire."

After she opened the trunk lid, Rolly delivered more bad news.

"Uhhhh…Nikki, I'm afraid your spare tire is flat, too." She dropped her shoulders, puffed out her bottom lip, and made a face like a third grader who was just told to go to the principal's office. Rolly said, "I'll tell you what. It's ok, we can run up town and get another tire."

She replied, "I'm so sorry to put you through this."

"Nah, it's ok, but why don't you wait inside my truck while I jack the car up and take the wheel off. We're gonna need to take it with us." She retreated to his truck as requested. He removed the ruined tire and took it, along with the spare tire.

They headed for a local tire shop that he was familiar with. During the short drive, they reintroduced themselves to each other more completely. After arriving at the tire shop, Nikki discovered her troubles weren't quite over. Two new tires were mounted on the rims without a problem. However, then it was time to pay out. Both of her cards were declined…twice. Rolly never hesitated. He pulled his card out of his wallet and offered to pick up the bill.

"I can't let you do that," she pleaded.

"Don't worry about it, it's ok."

"No, really, please don't."

"Nikki, right now we really don't have a choice…right?"

"I guess not. I'm sorry, I'm really sorry."

With two new tires loaded up and ready, they were back on their way. As they drove across town Rolly asked, "Have you eaten? I'm about to die. Do you have time to make a quick stop?"

She said, "I don't have anywhere to be."

What he didn't know was she was now in the early stages of developing a serious crush on this knight in shining armor who had rescued her and saved the day. She wanted to spend more time with him. He pulled into a Sonic drive-in. As they waited on their orders, she started the conversation. She first wanted to know what kind of work he did. He explained it all. She then inquired about how he knew her mother. He almost swallowed his tongue. He just told her they met once at the hospital and prayed she didn't ask anything else about that. Then she noticed the scar on his hand.

"How did what happen?" She pointed and said, "The scar on your hand."

"Oh that, well, I was being stupid and put my hand somewhere it didn't belong. A gate smashed it."

"Ouch…betcha won't do that again."

"No ma'am I won't."

"Now, that's funny."

He looked over and asked, "What's funny, my hand?"

"No, you called me ma'am."

"Oh, I'm sorry, I'm just trying to be polite."

"I like that. Guys who are polite are getting hard to find."

At this point he knew she was flirting with him and it made him extremely uncomfortable because of the secret he was hiding. Still, he was enjoying the conversation and her bubbly personality. After the burgers and fries were delivered, he continued the conversation.

"So, you go to school in San Angelo, huh?"

"How did you know that?"

"I saw the sticker in your window."

"Yep…big SA."

He proudly said, "I graduated from there."

"Oh really, when?"

"2003, I played football there a couple of years."

"Well, looky here, we just met and already we found something we have in common. We are both Rams!" Nikki then cut to the chase and asked the all-important question, "Are you married?"

He shook his head and said, "Nope."

She pried further, "Are you talking to anyone?"

He looked over at her to closely study her face. Was this a trap? Did she know something? He cautiously replied, "No…guess I don't have time for that right now." They finished their food and the conversation trailed off to the task at hand. "We better get going."

"Yeah, I hope my car is still there."

He laughed out loud and said, "Something tells me it ain't went anywhere."

He made her stay in his truck again as he worked. As he did, she rifled through a stack of his mail sitting on the dash. She covertly added his address into her phone. She already had his number saved. As she watched him she only became more enamored. She thought to herself, "How soon can I have another flat tire?" When her car was ready again, he jumped back inside his truck with her.

"Well, I guess you're ready to go."

"Rolly, I can't thank you enough. I don't know what I would have done. Daddy is flying and my mom is out of town, too." He stopped to contemplate what she just said. The part about mom being out of town gave him pause. It reminded him that Jess had clearly told him she had to work that day. At any rate, he assured Nikki that she was very welcome. She wasn't finished.

"I want to repay you for the tires and the lunch."

"That's not necessary."

"Yes, it is, and I insist. Can I buy your lunch one day soon?"

He felt his heart skip a beat. Any other place, any other time, he would have jumped at an offer like this from such a pretty girl. But she wasn't just another pretty girl. He felt dirty with feelings of guilt because of the secret he shared with her mother. He did not like being a liar. He just finally broke down and clumsily said, "Uhhhhh…yeah, ok…I guess that'll work."

"Ok, it's a deal. I'm going to call you."

"Alright, then."

He walked her to her car and stood by as she safely got back on the interstate and drove away. He couldn't deny the attraction he had for her. He realized then he had just been on a very good date, albeit short and unscheduled. He reached for his phone and sent a text to Jess.

"All systems go, she's back on the road."

Later that afternoon, Jess arrived back home to find her daughter sitting on the couch eating chips and watching T.V. Jess said, "Well, I see you made it home in one piece."

"Yes, but I don't know how. Where have you been today?" Jess lied and said, "I went to Lubbock with Tonya."

"What was going on there?"

"We just did some shopping and went out to eat."

"Where is Dad? When will he be back?"

"He had a flight to Denver. He'll be back tomorrow. Hey, I thought you were going to the game tonight."

"Yeah, Melissa is on her way to get me."

Jess noticed Nikki seemed to be in a very good mood and sensed that she had something she wanted to talk about. Jess opened the door to conversation by sitting down next to her daughter and asking, "So, did you get your flat tire fixed?"

Nikki's eyes widened, as did her smile. "Yes! Thanks for sending help."

Even though she already knew the answer, Jess asked, "Did Rolly get everything put back together?"

"Oh, he did more than that."

"What do you mean? What did he do?"

"Well, my tire couldn't be fixed so I had to get a new one. My debit card got declined, wouldn't you know it. Rolly paid for the tire and a new rim. Then he took me to lunch."

"Took you to lunch?"

"Well, not really lunch but we stopped to get a bite."

Jess' blood pressure began to rise but she just sat quietly.

"So, anyway, yeah he fixed everything and got me going again. Mom, how do you know him?"

"Who, Rolly?"

"Yes, Rolly...how do you know him?"

Jess, needing another white lie, came up with one. "I really don't know him. He is just a guy that does maintenance work at the hospital. I didn't know anyone else to call to go help you so I just asked him if he could do it."

Nikki retorted, "He doesn't do maintenance there, he works for Spurling."

"Oh yeah, that's right, but he used to be at the hospital and I still had his number."

"Well, I have his number now!"

Jess took one look at the glow on Nikki's face and knew there was a potential problem brewing.

"Nikki, don't get mixed up with that guy."

"Why? He's perfect. He has a good job. He is nice, and he's not married."

"Nikki, he is lot older than you."

"He doesn't look it." Young Nikki's smile got even wider and brighter now.

"I'm just telling you, he's not someone you want to get involved with."

"Why do you say that? Is there something about him you're not telling me?"

"No, Nikki, there's not, but there is just a lot of oil field trash around this town. I just want you to be careful."

"Mom, I'm not in the sixth grade. I can think for myself."

Jess reached over and gave her daughter's hand a supportive squeeze then got up to go find her cell phone. She now had a lot to say and needed to make a call.

Locked in her bathroom, sitting on the side of the tub, she called him. When Rolly answered she blurted out, "What the hell are you doing?"

"What are you talking about?"

"I'm talking about my daughter, that's what I'm talking about."

"What about her? I went and got her off the side of the highway like you asked me to do."

"Yes, and then what?"

"Jess, why don't you say whatever it is you gotta say, cuz I'm lost."

"It sounds to me like ya'll went and had a high time after changing a tire."

"Did she tell you what happened?"

"Oh yeah, she told me about dinner and everything."

Rolly, now in a defensive posture, said, "Wait just a damn minute, Jess. I ain't taking an ass chewing over something I didn't do. You called me at lunch time and I hadn't eaten a thing. It took me fifteen minutes to get to her. Her tire and the rim were ruined so I had to get a new one. All that took an hour and a half to find. So, excuse me for stopping long enough to eat a hamburger at a drive-in. And, what was I going to do, eat in front of her? She said she was hungry, too."

Jess suddenly felt terrible. It was obvious now she didn't have the whole story before sticking both feet in her mouth. But after a pause, she said, "Ok, let's start this over."

Rolly replied, "That would be a great idea."

"First, thank you for helping her, but there may be an issue now."

"What issue?"

"You must have made quite an impression on Nikki. She seems to have her eye on you now. If I know my daughter, you haven't heard the last of her."

"Are you kidding me?"

"No, I'm not. And Rolly, I have already lied to her about how I know you. If she starts asking questions you better deny until you die."

"Hey, I'm sorry if I caused a problem. I was just trying to help."

"No, no, no Rolly, I'm the one who owes you an apology. I shouldn't have assumed stuff before I had the story. So, I'm sorry."

"Apology not needed but accepted."

There was laughter on both ends of the call. Jess then wondered out loud, "Hey, I just had a thought. Did we just have our first fight?"

"I guess so. Is that progress? If so, I'll take it."

"You're silly. Hey, I'm getting another call I need to take. I'll catch you later."

"Ok, bye."

After ending the call, he paused long enough to rewind the conversation in his brain. Especially the part about Nikki having her eye on him. He was flattered.

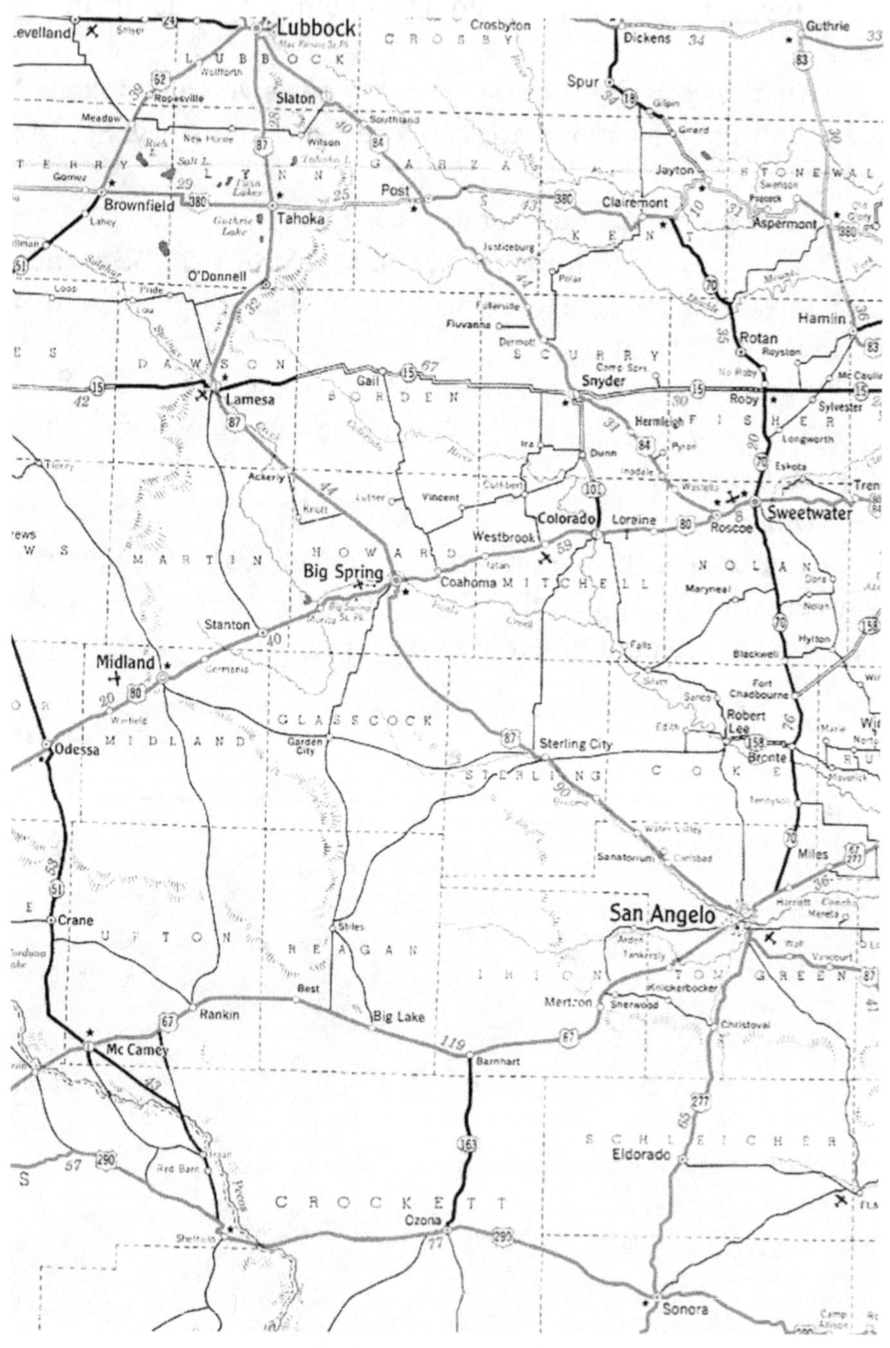
Levelland
Lubbock
Crosbyton
Dickens
Guthrie
Spur
Ropesville
Slaton
Meadow
New Home
Southland
Wilson
Jayton
Clairemont
Aspermont
Brownfield
Tahoka
Post
Justiceburg
O'Donnell
Fluvanna
Hamlin
Rotan
Dermott
Snyder
Lamesa
Gail
Hermleigh
Roby
Sylvester
Longworth
Ira
Dunn
Pyron
Estota
Ackerly
Luther
Vincent
Colorado
Loraine
Sweetwater
Knott
Westbrook
Roscoe
Big Spring
Coahoma
Stanton
Maryneal
Nolan
Blackwell
Midland
Germania
Falls
Odessa
Garden City
Sterling City
Fort Chadbourne
Robert Lee
Bronte
Crane
Stiles
Miles
San Angelo
Best
Ardon
Mertzon
Sherwood
Knickerbocker
Rankin
Big Lake
Christoval
Mc Camey
Barnhart
Eldorado
Red Barn
Ozona
Sheffield
Sonora

CHAPTER 7

IT WAS A SATURDAY AFTERNOON and Rolly was sitting on the sofa taking in the fourth quarter of the Longhorn game. It looked as though the Longhorns were gonna deal the Sooners an ass whippin' two years in a row. Suddenly, he got an incoming call from one of his guys on the number 2 crew.

"What's up, Manny?"

"Rolly, I need help, man."

"Where are you? what's wrong?"

"I'm at the Oasis Club. I'm hurt, can you come get me?"

"Yeah, I'm on my way. I'll be there in fifteen minutes. Are you good 'til then?"

"Come around the back when you get here."

Manny was his best field hand. He knew from the distress in his voice something was bad wrong. He wasted no time in getting to him. The bar he was headed to was a notorious trouble spot. After pulling into the parking lot, Rolly made his way around to the side of the building to the back. There he saw Manny's old white pickup sitting at the opposite corner near some dumpsters. The tailgate was down and Manny was laying across it. When Rolly stepped out of his truck, he was shocked at what he saw. Manny's shirt was blood-soaked. His face was also covered in blood and his right eye was swollen and completely shut. His lips were busted and his forehead had a large knot in the center.

"Manny, what happened to you? Who did this to you?"

Manny rolled off the tailgate and attempted to stand straight as he said, "A fucking Mexican beat my ass and he took my money."

"Who is he? Do you know him? Where did he go?"

"He left. I don't know who he is, but I've seen him before."

"Do you need to go to the hospital?"

"No, but I need a ride to my house. He threw my keys on top of the building."

Rolly helped Manny climb up inside his truck. He left the bar and drove to Manny's house. On the way, Manny told him the whole story. He had been playing pool for money with a big guy he had just met. They were betting one hundred bucks per game. Manny had won three in a row, but the big guy had failed to pay up and kept insisting on playing double or nothing. Finally, Manny demanded to be paid his winnings before playing another game. But he explained, "He told me he needed to go to his truck and get more money. I followed him outside so he wouldn't just drive off. That's when he jumped me from behind and beat me. He took all my money out of my wallet and threw my truck keys on the roof."

When they pulled into his gravel driveway, Manny bailed out and went inside while Rolly waited. A few minutes later he came back carrying a set of keys… and a big pistol.

"What are you gonna do with that?"

"I'm gonna kill that motherfucker!"

"You can't Manny, he ain't worth going to prison for."

"Do you expect me to let him beat me and rob me and do nothing?"

"No, we can get something done."

"Oh, really… what? I can't go to the police, I'll probably be the one who gets sent back."

"No Manny, but there is a better way."

"Ok, tell me."

"You have to trust me, but I will tell you now. Manny you ain't getting your money back, just a whole lot of satisfaction."

"Ok, then I trust you."

"Did you say you had seen him before?"

"Yeah, I think he has a welding shop. I've seen his truck at that shop over on Hightower Road before."

Rolly drove across town. They were looking for a green Dodge flatbed with a welding rig on the back. Passing by Cesar Gomez's welding shop, Manny was proven to be very observant. There sat the rig they were looking for. And as luck would have it, the owner of the truck was talking to another man nearby.

"There he is! That's him!"

"Are you sure, Manny? One hundred percent sure?"

'Yes, yes… that's the guy right there."

"Ok then, no problem."

They drove on past and then back to the Oasis to pick up Manny's truck. Before parting ways, Rolly told Manny, "I'll pick you up at your house at 10 o'clock.

"See you then, mejo," was all Manny said.

Rolly drove away and back to the ranch. Grabbing a bite to eat first, he then lay across the sofa. In his mind he went over the details of the plan he had formulated for later that night. However, it wasn't long before these thoughts and all others were pushed out of the way by thoughts of Jess. Where is she? What is she doing? Who is she with? It was enough to drive him insane. Finally, sleep saved him from a full-blown panic attack. It was a short nap though, as the ringer he had set on his phone began to tell him it was time to get moving. He threw on a heavy jacket, retrieved a cigarette lighter from the kitchen cabinet and walked out the door carrying an empty plastic bottle. At the ranch workshop he filled the plastic bottle half full with gasoline from the bulk tank. He started the truck and left on a mission.

Manny was ready and waiting for his friend to arrive. He hopped in and said, "Let's go!" Not a word was spoken as the two friends made the second trip over to Hightower Road. Driving slowly past the welding shop, they confirmed that their target was still there.

The business was closed so no one was round. Rolly casually made the statement, "It sure would be unfortunate if something were to happen to that pretty green Dodge truck."

Manny was completely unaware of what was coming next and asked, "What do we do?"

Rolly pulled into an alley on the opposite side of the street a half block away. Reaching underneath the seat he pulled out the plastic bottle containing the gasoline. He handed it, along with the lighter, to Manny. "Go get your satisfaction, partner, I'll wait here."

Without hesitation, Manny took the items, exited the truck, and jogged away into the darkness. It was two minutes later when Rolly saw the bright flash and the flames. Moments later, the passenger door flew open wide and in jumped Manny. Rolly shifted into drive, and they slowly rolled away down the alley. Manny couldn't contain himself. "That son of a bitch will be walking tomorrow!"

Rolly looked over at his friend and asked, "Well, was this a better way?"

A wide grin broke across Manny's battered face. "Eres un hombre sabio!" Yes, this was a much better way.!"

Rolly dropped Manny off at his front door with an offer and some good advice. He handed him a one-hundred-dollar bill and said, "Hey man, you can take a couple days off if you need to. I'll cover you." As Manny turned away, Rolly said, "Oh and Manny…I'd stay out of any bars for a while." Manny leaned into the cab for a hand shake, then Rolly drove away.

CHAPTER 8

IT WAS MID-OCTOBER and Rolly was about to get Jake for an entire week. He wanted everything to be perfect for his son. He asked to take the week off from work. Hoss was fully aware of the situation and didn't hesitate to give him the time he needed. Rolly had an idea and was hoping to kill two birds with one stone. The Midland County Fair was starting on Friday. Jake, at five years of age had never experienced a fair, the circus, a zoo, or much else. Rolly hoped to change all that starting now.

He also wanted to introduce Jess to his young son. It had been a couple of weeks since he had seen her face, and he was hoping to talk her into tagging along. His text messages over the next two days went unanswered. He didn't try to call her because she'd warned him not to do that for fear there might be others listening. He didn't know whether to be irritated or worried. He was beginning to be a little of both. Finally, on Monday morning he got a text.

"Hey."

"Hey. Where in the world have you been, I was getting worried."

"No biggie, I was in Fort Worth."

"What was going on there?"

"I had to go check on my mom."

"What was wrong with her?"

"She just had a little spell, she's ok now."

"Are you still off on Fridays?"

"Yeah, what's up?"

"I've got Jake all week and the fair starts Friday. I want to take him. Go with us."

"Ok, let's do that."

"Great." They did some more catching up over the phone before agreeing to meet at the ranch at noon on Friday. He had a busy workweek and the days seemed to fly by.

Friday at lunch her black Mercedes showed up at the ranch right on schedule. Rolly was in the yard trying to teach Jake how to pitch horseshoes, without much luck. After introductions all three of them loaded into Rolly's truck and headed for Midland. After burgers in town, they arrived at the crowded fairgrounds. Jake was disappointed that he was too small for most of the rides on the Midway, but he loved the carousel.

During his third trip on the wooden horses, a young woman walked up behind Jess and tapped her on the shoulder. Jess turned and immediately recognized her and started a cheerful conversation. Rolly remained quiet and directed all his attention on his son. A couple of minutes later the young woman gave Jess a big hug, looked over at Rolly with a smile and walked away into the crowd. Feeling like a kid caught red-handed with a hand in the cookie jar Rolly asked, "Are we in trouble?"

"Nah…it's all good."

"Who was that?"

"She's a nurse I used to work with on nights."

"Oh hell."

"It was bound to happen, but you know what?"

"What?"

"I don't really care."

The ride ended and Jake then reminded his dad that he loved funnel cakes. Later, on the way to the truck they made one last stop to attempt to win a stuffed bear. Rolly spent thirty bucks and almost threw his shoulder out chunking baseballs before he finally got the job done. Prized bear now in hand, Jake was ready to head back to the ranch. Travelling down the interstate Rolly and Jess were revisiting the encounter with the young woman from earlier. Then, from the car seat in the back Jake demanded, "Turn on the music."

Jess punched the on button and asked, "What kind of music do you like, Jake?"

He shouted, "Uncle Kracker!" The laughter that followed lasted more than a mile. Once again Jake spoke up from his car seat. "Jess, are you my daddy's girlfriend?"

Jess paused with a blank look on her face. She and Rolly traded glances at each other. She then put on a smile, turned and said, "Jake, your daddy is a very good friend of mine. We like each other very much." Hearing those words she spoke sent the blood in Rolly's body rushing to his feet. She had a chance to say it. She had a chance to make it real, but she passed.

It was dark and Jake was asleep when they got back to the guest house. Rolly carried him in and put him down for the night. In the kitchen, Jess poured two glasses of iced tea. They sat down together on the couch and Jess kicked off her shoes. They spent an hour just quietly talking. He listened to every word she said but he was distracted. Thoughts of kissing her were racing through his mind. He had waited long enough and was waiting for a sign, an opportunity, the right words, anything that told him it was time.

He never received any such indication that the time was right. Instead, she said, "I guess I'd better get going." She stood up and began to slip her feet inside her shoes. Standing close beside her, he made his move. Rolly put his hands around the back of her arms and pulled her to him. She didn't resist and just stared into his eyes. That was it. He slowly leaned forward, directing his lips toward hers. At the very last possible second, she turned her head away and his kiss landed squarely on the side of her face. Turning back to him she apologized, "I'm sorry, I'm just not ready."

Disappointed, he walked her to her car and thanked her for spending the day with him and his son.

CHAPTER 9

MOST OF NOVEMBER came and went. Rolly got really busy guiding hunters and entertaining other invited guests at the ranch on weekends. The oil field didn't offer him many breaks, either. His free time was practically nonexistent.

Jess and Curtis continued to tolerate each other, but the trajectory of their marriage was taking a noticeable nose-dive. However, neither one was ready to give up yet. Nikki began preparing herself for the Fall final exams. Only the Spring semester was left and then he would be out in the real world. Although she had a lot on her plate, with clinicals and tests, she hadn't forgotten about Rolly and her desire to repay him for his good deeds. During her Thanksgiving break she found herself holding two tickets for a show featuring a very popular country band that was playing in Odessa. This is what she had been waiting for. She went looking for him and she wasn't taking no for an answer.

She showed up at the ranch just before noon on that Saturday. Rolly heard Gus going crazy and he went to the window. He thought, "Who the hell is this?" A small car was slowly driving in a circle between the main lodge and the guest house. Then he realized he was familiar with this particular car. Nikki spotted him just as he walked out the door. He stepped off the wooden porch and met her at the driver's side door as she was getting out. She burst out of the car with a huge smile on her face.

"Hello, Rolly Burnett!"

"Hey girl, what are you doing here?"

"Gosh, you don't seem excited to see me."

"No, I am, but how did you find this place?"

"I have a confession. I looked at your mail in your truck."

"I see, well here you are, what's up?"

"Guess what? I have two tickets to see Rowdy Reeves and the Plainsmen in Odessa tonight."

Rolly knew the band and liked their music a lot. "Wow, that's cool."

"Yeah, and guess what else. You and I are going!"

"Tonight???"

"Yes, tonight."

"Nikki wait, listen, I can't go. I've got a lot going on today."

"Nope, don't even try to say no. I told you I was going to repay you for what you did and tonight's the night."

Slowly shaking his head side to side he said, "I really can't."

Her beautiful smile wilted into a look of desperation, "Please Rolly, please?"

He stared at her as he thought of her mother. He was feeling sick to his stomach. He had learned his lesson a long time ago and knew a man's lies always catch up with him. Right now, his lies were right on his heels. She was dressed perfectly. Makeup, perfect. Hair, perfect. Obviously, she had put forth time and effort to be standing here in front of him. He didn't have the heart to say no.

"Alright then I guess I can get one of the cowboys to take care of everything here." Her face regained its glow. Rolly asked her, "What time does the show start?"

"It starts at eight, but I thought we would eat first."

He wanted to know, "What are we gonna do between now and then? That's about six hours we need to kill."

She advised him, "Well, I've got to run to Midland to fill out some paperwork at the clinic. I'm applying for an internship there. But then, I'll come pick you up."

"Uhhhh…no, thank you. I'll drive, I don't trust your tires."

Laughing she gave him a bear hug and said, "I'll be back at five, ok?"

"I'll be here."

Then suddenly her excitement was replaced by a serious tone. "Rolly, there is one thing, you can't ever say anything about this to my mom."

He froze and cautiously asked, "Ok, but why is that?"

She explained, "Cause for some reason, I don't think she likes you and I don't want her in my business."

That night at the tavern, after a splendid dinner, they laughed, they danced, they sang, and they drank. All to the sound of live music. To anyone watching, who didn't know better, Rolly and Nikki looked like the perfect couple. But finally, the last call went out and the party was about to end after one more slow dance.

As they slowly made their way around the dance floor, she asked him, "When do you plan on kissing me?" In a panic, he leaned forward and gave her a quick, very unromantic kiss on the lips. Her disappointment was very obvious. Then the drinks stopped flowing, the music stopped, and he was back to reality. He was in a mess. Rolly was caught in the middle between a woman that he wanted and another woman that desperately wanted him. To complicate matters, these two women knew each other extremely well and had for a long, long time.

Nikki was noticeably quiet on the way back to the ranch. When they got there, it was late but she wasn't in a hurry to get out of his truck. "Hey, can we talk?"

Shrugging his shoulders he replied, "Sure, is everything ok?"

"I don't know. I'm confused, I guess."

"About what?"

"You…I'm trying to figure you out but I can't. All night I've been getting this feeling that you needed to say something."

Rolly said, "I don't understand."

Nikki asked, "Did you have a good time tonight?"

Laughing, he replied, "Hell yes, I did. Thanks for everything."

Then she wondered out loud, "You're not attracted to me, are you?"

He knew exactly what was causing her confusion. Here she was, a beautiful single girl practically throwing herself at him, but he was holding back. She wanted to know why. He took his cowboy hat off and pitched it up on the dash and leaned back in the seat.

"Nikki, I'm sorry. I did have a great time tonight. I had a blast. There's just something I'm dealing with. It has nothing to do with you."

"Well, what is it? You can talk to me."

"No, I can't…I just can't."

Curious, she asked, "You're seeing someone aren't you? Why didn't you just tell me?"

"Well, I guess I am, but not really."

"That's the stupidest thing I've ever heard a guy say! You either are, or you're not."

"Ok, I am, I just need time to work things out."

Disgusted, she said, "I just wish you would have told me so I wouldn't have wasted your time or mine."

"Wasted your time? Is that what I did?"

"Rolly, are you playing stupid or something? It ain't funny. I'm not making it a big secret that I like you." He just stared down at his boots. She prodded him, "Don't you have anything to say?"

"Yes, actually I do. You know what you said earlier today about not telling your mom about tonight?"

"Yeah, so what?"

"Nikki, you can't tell her about any of this."

"For God's sake! I told you I wasn't going to say anything to her and you'd better not either. What is it with you two? Y'all act so weird. Y'all are just alike."

She got out of his truck and walked over to her car. He followed close behind. Just as she was about to get inside, he grabbed her arm and turned her to him. He then kissed her the way she wanted to be kissed. Then he told her, "Nikki, listen to me. I had one of the best times of my life tonight. I want you to know that and believe it. Thank you very much. I'm just in a complicated situation right now. Would you please stay in touch with me?"

She seemed to accept his explanation. She smiled and simply said, "Ok." After getting inside her car, she rolled down the window and smirked, "Hey, we're even now, I paid you back."

He just smiled as she drove away into the night.

CHAPTER 10

THE BIG COUNTRY got its first snow of the winter and Christmas was only three weeks away. Tonya's big holiday bash was only days away. Jess had a lot on her mind that she needed to discuss with her close friend. Her secrets were becoming harder to keep. On a coffee break in the hospital cafeteria, she dropped a bombshell.

"Tonya, I need to talk about something. Curtis isn't coming to the Christmas party."

"I knew that. You already told me."

"There's more. Tonya, I'm going to ask Curtis for a divorce."

Tonya covered her ears with her hands and pursed her lips together tightly upon hearing those words. "Oh my God, Jess, has something happened?"

"No nothing happened but, I just can't take it anymore. We're done. Both of us know it."

"Have you told him yet?"

"No! And I don't want it to get out. I'm waiting until after the first of the year when Nikki goes back to school. I don't want this to screw up Christmas for her and the rest of our family."

Tonya sighed and dropped her shoulders saying, "Ok, yeah, I get that. I'm so sorry, Jess. I hate to hear all this."

"Don't be. I'm actually relieved. Now I need to tell you something else and get your permission."

"My permission? What on earth are you talking about?"

"I want to bring someone else to the party with me."

"Ohhhhh…you wanna bring Michael, right?"

"No, Tonya, it's someone else."

Tonya's forehead wrinkled up a bit and her head tilted slightly when she asked, "Who is it? Do I know him?"

"I've started seeing someone else and you met him once, kinda, I guess."

"Stop playing me, tell me who it is."

"Do you remember last summer on the trip back from Fort Worth when we were at the truck stop and that guy came up…" Tonya interrupted by cutting her off in mid-sentence.

"Oh my God, the guy at the truck stop! Please tell me you are fucking kidding me!"

"Would you please keep your voice down?"

Almost in a whisper Tonya asked, "Jess, are you sitting here telling me that you have been dating that guy? You sure have some explaining to do."

"I know, I know. It's a long story and I'll tell you everything, but I want to bring him. Is it ok?"

"Of course it is, but what's going on with you and Michael? Are ya'll on the outs, too?"

"No, no, no we're fine. Nothing's changed."

"Really, Jess? How are you able to get away with all this?"

"It's not easy. But please Tonya, don't say anything to anyone please. I just needed to talk to someone."

"You know I wouldn't say a word. I'm not your ride-or-die for nothing."

On the day of the party Rolly agreed to pick up Jess at her house. She jumped inside his truck and quickly gave him a kiss. She was a sight to see in her new red and white Christmas dress. He was blown away. "Wow, look at you."

In an almost childish manner she arched her shoulders, smiled, closed her eyes and asked, "You like?"

"Yes, I like…very much. What is that you got with ya?" Jess was holding a colorful package in her hand. "Santa Clause sent you something. He asked me to give it to you." She then handed him a small, gift-wrapped box. He shook it, then with a wide grin held it up to his ear.

"What is it?"

"Well, open it silly."

He said, "I hate surprises."

"Ok, then give it back. She playfully grabbed at the box but he pulled it away.

"No way," he said as he began to tear into the paper. When he opened it, his eyes fixed on the shiny object inside and he fell silent. Inside the box, lying on fine grain felt, was a beautiful belt buckle with the engraved title BAREBACK CHAMPION 2003. Below the title was his name, ROLAND JAMES BURNETT.

"Do you like it?"

He just looked at her for a few seconds with his mouth hanging open, before asking, "How much did you pay for this?"

"That's none of your business, but I will tell you it's hand made. Do you like it?"

"I love it, thank you."

"I thought you might…you've just about worn your old one smooth."

Rolly protested, "Dammit, Jess, why didn't you tell me we were giving gifts? I didn't bring you anything."

"Oh, shut up, there's plenty of shopping days 'til Christmas."

He drove out of the parking lot, and they headed to the country club outside town for what would be a very eventful Christmas party.

They arrived fashionably late. A crowd of about fifty friends and co-workers were already gathered in the banquet room. Tonya and her boyfriend Frank met Jess and Rolly at the door. Jess was happy to see her friend but Frank, not so much. Frank, one year earlier, had actually chased Jess with the single goal of getting in her pants. When she wouldn't give him the time of day, he settled for her best friend.

Tonya had told Frank that Jess would be bringing a surprise guest. His jealousy would be evident immediately. Jess introduced Rolly to both of them. Rolly recalled the less than warm reception he had received from Tonya six months before. But, without worries, he smiled and extended his hand. Tonya shook his hand warmly.

When it was Frank's turn, he grabbed Rolly's hand a little too firmly and said, "Jess, this is a Christmas party, not bring your son to work day."

This wisecrack led Jess to say, "Oh, Frank shut up."

Both women rolled their eyes and walked into the room. Frank's stupid remark also landed him in the center of Rolly's radar. For the next two hours a good time was had by all. Rolly, being good at conversation, blended in well and everyone treated him like a long-time member of the group. Everyone except Frank. Tonya, being the hostess, stayed busy trying to entertain everyone. It was her party and she wanted it to be perfect. While she was busy keeping the food trays stocked and refilling drinks, Frank used the time to follow Jess and her date around. The more he drank, the worse his low-level harassment became. He made several remarks such as "That dress makes you look like a Christmas package I would really like to unwrap" and "Hey,

Jess, later I need you to help me with my Christmas list". But most of his drunken juvenile remarks were directed at Rolly.

Near sunset, most of the partygoers had left. The handful that remained started to gather outside near a warm fire at the burn pit. As Jess left Tonya in the kitchen area, she walked to the exit door. Through the glass she saw Frank saying something to Rolly. Rolly's body language told her he wasn't enthused at hearing anything else Frank had to say. Jess quietly walked over to Frank and whispered to him, "Frank, would you please lay off Rolly…for me, please lay off?"

Rather than grant her request, he foolishly went the total opposite direction. Frank stood up and abruptly declared, "Jess you know I've always been there for ya, baby. I'll prove it." He then walked over and stood face to face with Rolly. "Young man I'm going to get us all another drink. Can I get you a Root Beer or something?"

In the blink of an eye the smartass was lying on the ground having been punched in the face by a very pissed off Roland James Burnett. His shoulder blades had no sooner hit the concrete floor before Rolly put the bottom of his boot across the right side of Frank's face, pinning the left side to the ground. There was a deafening silence all around as Rolly, in a low, demanding voice asked, "Who is your daddy?"

Jess yelled at him, "Stop it right now!"

Ignoring her, he again demanded, "You tell me, who is your daddy."

Through bloody lips Frank muttered the words, "You are."

With the satisfaction he was looking for having been gained, Rolly turned and headed for his truck. He never looked back but told Jess loudly, "We're leaving, get in the truck."

The small crowd of onlookers was in a state of shock at what they had just witnessed. Tonya, suddenly back on the scene, held up her phone and threatened to call the police. Jess confronted her with, "Here's a better idea...tell Frank to man up."

Rolly was waiting with the engine running when Jess crawled up into the truck and demanded to know, "What in the hell was that back there?"

"I got tired of his damn mouth."

"I'm not talking about him. I'm talking about me, dammit!"

"What about you?"

"I'll tell you what the fuck about me Rolly Burnett. You don't get to tell me when to get in the truck. You don't get to tell me what truck to get into. And you don't get to embarrass me in front of my friends and then turn your back on me and walk away. Now, take me to my car."

Dead silence filled the cab of the truck for the next twenty long minutes. He hadn't planned on this and didn't want the night to end in this way. He was still pissed but beginning to feel guilty. Her silence was driving him crazy. He thought to himself that arguing would be better than this. Finally, Rolly decided to try and break the ice. "Jess, I'm sorry. I shouldn't have done what I did. I shouldn't have hit him, ok?"

She had now calmed down herself and said, "Forget it. I was about ready to punch him myself. You just better hope he doesn't decide to file charges on you."

Rolly wondered, "Do you think he will?"

"Probably not. Hopefully, when he sobers up, he'll realize what an ass he was being to everyone."

Sensing a possible truce, Rolly asked, "Do you still wanna go to your car?"

"No, I don't. Take me to a bar, I need a drink."

Relieved about her sudden change in attitude, Rolly cut across to Colorado City to a familiar watering hole there. The couple parked the truck and made their way inside. The Frosty

Hog Saloon was always packed on Saturday nights and this Saturday was no different. The dance floor was full of cowboys and cowgirls two stepping to loud country music.

After that first drink, Jess and Rolly joined them. The music put smiles on two faces that needed a change of pace. The smiles were soon replaced by laughter. After a few dances it seemed that the unfortunate incident earlier in the day was now a distant memory. But, not quiet. After the music stopped and they returned to their seats at the bar, Jess had one more question about the previous events. She took a long drink from her glass, turned to Rolly and asked, "Hey, today did you hit Frank because of the things he said to you, or because of the things he said to me?"

"Both."

"I mean, were you jealous today?"

He answered, "Yeah, honestly, I guess I was. And I'll tell you something else. The truth is, if I had to do it all over…I'd hit him again. You mean more to me than you know."

She just stared at him for a brief moment then finished what was left in her glass. She got up from her stool and wrapped her arms around his neck. She whispered in his ear, "Let's get out of here."

They left the honky-tonk and got back on the interstate highway headed west. Not much time had passed when Jess sent out that unmistakable signal he had been waiting on for so long. In the darkness she reached over to his arm resting on the center console. Her fingertips slowly glided down his forearm to his hand. She took his hand in hers and interlocked her fingers through his. He knew the time had finally arrived. No more words were spoken as they drove through the night to the ranch. No more words were needed.

Chapter 11

ARRIVING AT THE RANCH just before midnight, Rolly drove across the cattle guard, past the main lodge, and around to the guest house. Gus met them with a wagging tail as they got out of the truck. Rolly extended his hand to help Jess up onto the wooden porch with a warning, "Watch your step." She took his hand and pulled herself up onto the porch and pushed herself into his arms. He greeted her with a passionate kiss.

Their two worlds had collided now and were about to start spinning as one. He pitched the truck keys onto the kitchen table as he pulled her along, down the hallway to his bedroom. And now, after all the months of patiently waiting and against all the odds in the world, she is finally standing face to face with him in this dimly lit room. This scene has been coming for some time now, and neither has any doubt what they are here for.

He reaches out and grabs her waist with both hands and pulls her close. She doesn't resist. He leans in and she accepts a kiss… and then another. This is what he has been longing for. He can taste her breath now. She wraps her hands around his head and runs her fingers through his thick brown hair. He knows he has won. Then, as if they had rehearsed it a thousand times, they eagerly began to undress each other. He can feel a tide rising within himself. Now, less than half dressed, he takes her shoulders and begins to walk her backward. She reaches the bedside and can retreat no further. He pushes her back until she falls. She makes no effort to catch herself. Once on her back, Jess used her elbows to pull herself to the center of the bed. He follows her. Resting on his knees and elbows, Rolly has her pinned underneath him. She has now thrown off all caution and let loose all inhibition. It was a sweet surrender. Very slowly and gently, he begins to kiss her forehead. He uses his lips to explore all the features of her face and neck. He can feel the warmth of her hands as they slide up his sides and onto the center of his back. She closes her eyes and breathes deeply as his kisses continue lower and lower across all the creases and curves of her body. When he arrives at her navel, her smooth silky skin is tense. He hesitates just long enough to peel her panties off and remove his jeans. Then, he is laying back beside her. His kisses resume. No longer content with his progress, she takes his hand and guides it to her flower. He is surprised but pleased by the moisture that greets his fingertips as he explores each hidden petal. Her heartbeat quickens as she begins to lose control, completely unaware of the soft moans she is making. He hears them clearly, as an invitation to send her over the edge. He goes down to finish what he started. The warmth and softness of his lips pressed against that spot sends shockwaves through her body outward to her hands and feet. Her toes are curled and she is tightly clutching the pillows as her body suddenly becomes gripped in sheer ecstasy. A few seconds later, and much too soon, it was over. She took a moment to fully enjoy the gift she had just received, but then she took control. It was now his turn and she was more than willing and able to return the favor. The next ten minutes resembled a wrestling match as the pair constantly traded positions in a game of lust. Nothing was off-limits. Finally, however, he became eager to end this episode. Laying on top between her arms and legs, he penetrated deep inside her. Fully erect, he began to thrust himself forcefully, forward and back. He continued as he felt it coming. The muscles in his abdomen tightened in preparation. Stronger and stronger the spasms became until he could take it no longer. Breathless and trembling, he pulled away, and not a second too soon. Then it happened. That magical release that no words can describe. Jess took him in her hand and gently coaxed the last remaining drops of the pearly white pleasure out of his shaft. He collapsed face-down on the bed. After a minute or two, their silence turned into laughter which then turned into small talk. The couple lay wrapped around each other, whispering. With each passing moment the conversation became quieter and shorter. One-word questions were answered with one-word replies. Minutes turned into an hour then…they were asleep. Outside, it was a long, cold, dark night.

"HOLY SHIT!!"…He sat straight up in bed at the sudden sound of her voice. "Rolly, let's go! I have to go now!"

Rolling off both sides of the bed, they hurriedly began grabbing clothes that were scattered about on the floor. The sunlight shining through the crack in the curtains meant trouble. She should have been home hours ago. Curtis and Nikki were both due back at home that morning, if they weren't already there. No words were spoken as they got into his truck. He sensed she wasn't in the mood to talk. As he sped down the winding oil topped road toward town, he occasionally glanced over at her. Her blank stare straight ahead told him she was thinking, so he remained quiet. At the edge of town, she finally broke her silence and said, "Turn here."

Confused, he did what he was told but this wasn't the way to her car or her house. She continued to give directions to some unknown location, and for what purpose, he did not know. However, one more left turn onto a dead-end street, it all became clear. There, parked at the end of the street, was a vehicle he recognized. A white Dodge Challenger. The very same Challenger Jess had been riding shotgun in the first afternoon he met her. It was clear to him what was going on now. Jess needed cover and she knew exactly where to find it. Tonya…where else? She needed to talk to her anyway, about what had happened at the party. He pulled up to the curb. Her door was open before the truck even came to a complete stop. She grabbed her things and hopped out. Still unsure of her mood, he just sat there, lips sealed. She did one final clothes check, then looked straight at him. Now her expression changed. It became softer. Leaning back inside the passenger window she smiled at him and said, "I'll call you."

Feeling a little better now, he pulled away from the curb and drove away without looking back. The short drive back to the ranch never seemed so far. He just kept replaying the events from the previous night over and over in his head. Looking back over the past eight months, he could have never predicted, or even imagined the two of them would end up together in the way they had. Not only were they complete opposites in every way possible, but the age difference between them made it all the more unlikely. Not many 35-year-old guys end up dating 41-year-old women. Even less, end up dating 41-year-old married women with a 21-year-old daughter. Regardless, he felt like he was falling in love with her. He just kept thinking about all of it over and over. How did a chance encounter at a truck stop turn out like this? Pulling up to the front gate at the ranch he shifted the truck into park and just sat motionless. Several minutes went by and he began to daydream about that afternoon in late April when it all started.

His trip down memory lane was cut short by the sound of a pickup crossing the cattle guard behind him. He stepped out to have a short conversation with the driver. After sending the truck and driver on their way, he drove up to the main lodge where Hoss was standing on the front porch having a heated conversation with someone over the phone. Rolly overheard Hoss tell that someone, "I pay the bills around here so it's gonna happen on my timeline. Not yours. Now just do it."

After he hung up, Rolly asked Hoss, "Boss, is everything ok?"

"Yeah, everything's ok. Sometimes I just have to remind my business partner who owns this company. Hey, Rolly, who was that up at the front gate?"

"It was that guy from the wind farm company again. They want to do some kind of feasibility study."

"What did you tell him?"

"I told him what I figured you would tell him. I told him to get his ass off the property."

Hoss laughed out loud and exclaimed, "Now, see son, that's why I keep you around here."

Hoss slapped Rolly on the back and together they went inside where Maria had made their breakfast.

Back at Tonya's house, Jess was busy apologizing for how the Christmas party had ended. They were too close to let anything like that come between them. All was well. Jess then brought Tonya totally up to speed on her crazy mixed-up love life. It was as much a counseling session as it was an information update.

Chapter 12

JANUARY CAME AND WENT, and that winter turned out to be a bitter cold one with lots of ice and snow. The weather complicated his work in the oil field and Rolly also stayed very busy helping to maintain things at the ranch. It was muddy, sloppy work in both places.

Jess finally confronted Curts with her divorce decision. It came as a little bit of a surprise to her when he agreed to her terms without much debate. It was time now to advise her parents and Nikki of what was on the horizon. She knew no one in her family was going to take the news well, but she wasn't second guessing herself and wasn't looking back. She also needed to tell Rolly. The two of them hadn't seen a lot of each other since New Year's Day, when they took a long drive through the country. He was always working, and she had been out of town a lot. They had been maintaining their relationship mostly through constant text messages. Nikki and Rolly also kept in touch with an occasional text.

By the end of February Rolly was eager to be with Jess again and she needed to tell him about her plans, so they arranged to meet. He picked her up in front of the studio after the end of her dance class. They then drove to what was becoming a favorite spot to sit and talk, the boat ramp on Lake

Thomas. He lifted the center console so she could get comfortable next to him. For half an hour, they indulged in small talk and traded kisses.

During a quiet moment she finally felt the moment was right and she spoke up. "Rolly, I need to tell you something. Curtis and I are getting a divorce."

He immediately quit fiddling with the knobs on the radio and sat back in his seat. He spent a brief second or two soaking up the news she had just laid on him. Then he asked, "Is this because of me?"

"Haaaa," she laughed, "don't flatter yourself."

"Flatter myself? That's a hell of a thing to say to me. Damn, sometimes you're hateful."

"I'm sorry, I didn't mean it that way."

"Well, how else did you mean it?"

"No, it isn't because of you. It's been coming for a long time. I've told you about our situation. You know all of this."

"So, when is this gonna happen?"

"We've already filed. My understanding is it takes about 120 days to be finalized."

"What then?"

"We're selling the house."

"You're staying here though, right?"

"Yeah, for now, but I may be staying with Tonya some."

"What about Curtis, what is he gonna do?"

"I think he's going to Lubbock to get closer to the airport."

Rolly didn't know how to feel about the sudden changes coming. On one hand, he had feelings of guilt about possibly having a big hand in the breaking up of a marriage. On the other hand, he thought maybe this was a turning point that might allow them the freedom to get closer, and he told her as much. "Jess, if you're telling me I didn't cause this, then I believe you, but I can't help but believe that I had a part in it. That doesn't make me feel good."

"Rolly, don't overthink this, ok?"

"Ok then… what does this mean for us?"

"Listen, there is something else that you…" She stopped in mid-sentence and turned her head away and began looking out the passenger window.

He asked, "What? Tell me… what else."

She wanted to tell him but couldn't. She needed to confess but couldn't find the courage. Not now, she wasn't ready. Turning back to him, she said, "Never mind, forget it. It's nothing, but listen, I may be hard to get hold of for a while. I'm going to be busy."

Looking deep into her eyes… her lying eyes… he knew there was something else. He didn't press the issue and just said, "Ok." Without any further discussion, he drove her back to her car in town.

For the most part, it was an amicable split. In fact, Jess and Curtis hired the same divorce attorney to represent both of them. The saving's accounts were split down the middle. He kept his truck and payments, and she kept her car, along with the payments. She didn't mess with his 401K or future earnings, and he left hers alone, as well. They decided to sell the house and split the proceeds fifty-fifty. Personal items and furniture never became a big issue. They were not trying to hurt each other, quite the contrary. Really, they both just wanted out. Curtis agreed to let Jess stay in the house until it sold. He moved into a pilot friend's apartment in Lubbock, temporarily. However, six weeks later he was living with a woman who happened to be a stewardess. That told Jess all she needed to know and helped her to move quickly past any thoughts of regret.

CHAPTER 13

IN THE THREE WEEKS that had passed since she told him about her impending divorce, she had been very hard to get hold of, just as she had warned. Many of his texts to Jess went unanswered. Her work schedule at the hospital had apparently changed drastically. He knew because he often checked the parking lot there. Her car was gone when it should have been sitting there. She was obviously avoiding any face-to-face contact.

He knew getting a divorce was a traumatizing experience. He had been there before himself and knew all about it firsthand. He wanted to think that was what was going on and was willing to give her time and space. But there was something else. He couldn't put his finger on it, but his gut told him there was more going on than what little she was telling him.

Rolly was desperate to put things back like they were at Christmas. He felt like he might have a chance to do just that when he finally convinced her to accompany him to the San Angelo Stock Show Rodeo. The annual event there would be a sort of homecoming for him. He grew up near there and had ridden bucking horses in that arena many times. On the way to the coliseum, she didn't seem distant at all, like she had been over the last several weeks. She laughed and smiled a lot. The conversation was pleasant and even amorous at times. She was relaxed, having gotten the monkey off her back. No more sneaking around. She was free now to do as she pleased, with whoever, or whenever she wanted.

They took their seats along the front row on the east side of the packed arena. They watched as the finest cowboys and cowgirls in the land competed in the NFR qualifying events. After the barrel racing concluded, bulls began being loaded into the bucking chutes and there was a brief intermission. Rolly took the opportunity to ask his date, "I'm thirsty, do you want something to drink?"

"Yeah, ok I could use something. Just get me a Diet Coke if they have it. If not, anything will do."

"Okee-dokee, I'll be right back." He headed for the concession stand lines. Meanwhile, unknown to him, a very familiar face was already standing in line at the women's restroom. It was Nikki Chapman. Nikki and a friend of hers had decided to attend the rodeo weeks before. They weren't huge rodeo fans, but it was an opportunity to possibly meet eligible cowboys. Nikki entered the restroom just as Rolly took his place in line to get drinks. A few minutes later after taking care of her business, Nikki emerged from the ladies' room and began to weave her way back through the crowd toward her seat. She just happened to look over and see him.

The sight of Rolly standing at the counter immediately brought a smile to her face. She veered right in order to go over and surprise him. However, on the way over she noticed something. He was paying for two large drinks. Now suddenly she wondered who he was here with. She ducked back into the crowd with a plan to find out. After paying, Rolly collected his refreshments and headed back to his seat. Nikki was not far behind. Rolly handed Jess her drink and sat back down beside her. A short distance away stood Nikki. Her body went numb when she saw her mother and Rolly sitting together holding hands. In an instant, she realized she had been lied to by both of them. She felt like a fool.

Rolly and Jess were in the middle of a conversation when they both became aware of a presence standing in front of them. They looked up to see Nikki staring. She was silent and smiling. Then, she forcefully reached down and took the drink out of Rolly's hand. Now her expression changed from a smile to a devilish look that Lucifer himself would have been proud of. She shouted for everyone in the audience to hear, "YOU SICK PATHETIC BASTARD!" She launched the entire contents of the Styrofoam cup into his face, knocking off his hat in the process. She didn't say a single word to her mother. She would save all that for later.

Nikki disappeared as suddenly as she had arrived. Rolly and Jess just sat quiet and motionless. Both of them knew they deserved the embarrassment that they were currently suffering under. The couple got up and left the arena. This date was over.

Later that night, Jess walked through her front door to find Nikki blocking the hallway. "Wow Mom, really? When were you going to tell me?" Jess ducked her head and walked past her daughter down the hallway and into the kitchen. Nikki angrily followed her, looking for a confrontation.

"I'll say one thing for you, Mom, you have some flexible standards."

"Stop it, Nikki, I don't want to talk about this."

"Well I do, so we are."

"No, we are not, you wouldn't understand, anyway."

"What's so hard to understand? It's really simple, my mother has been fucking oil field trash."

Jess reacted suddenly and forcefully. With both hands covering her mouth, Nikki turned back to face her mother, stinging from the force of the slap across the face she had just received. As tears began to run down her cheeks, Jess had her finger pointed at her daughter.

"Young lady, you will not speak to me that way in my house. I have a lot going on in my life right now and none of it is good. I could use some space. I need some understanding, but I demand some respect. Do you understand me?"

Jess walked out of the kitchen and disappeared down the hallway. Nikki stood silently staring at the tile floor. She got her confrontation, but it wasn't anything like she'd expected. For the first time in her young life, she had a serious misunderstanding with her mother. She had the strange feeling something in their relationship had just been broken.

In her bedroom, Jess sat on the side of the bed deep in thought. Her emotions were on the verge of boiling over. She was already thinking about how to apologize to Nikki. What to do about Rolly was a close second. And then, of course, there was the big question. What to do about her most guarded secret.

Finally, it all became too much. She was tired of living a lie. She was tired of the roller coaster ride her life was becoming. She was tired and her brain needed a rest. She filled the bath with hot water as she undressed. As she submerged her body beneath the water, a sense of calm came over her. It was time to make some tough decisions, but she was ready now to make them. That thirty-minute soak became a baptism, of sorts. She would not be the same person when it was over.

PUBLIC
BOAT RAMP
TEXAS DEPARTMENT OF TRANSPORTATION

CHAPTER 14

THE NEXT MORNING, Jess awoke to find that Nikki had already left and was on her way back to San Angelo. She poured her morning coffee and sat at the kitchen bar thinking about the day ahead. After her thoughts were organized, she picked up the phone and texted Rolly. For the first time ever, she invited him to her home. A hydraulic leak on a tractor prevented him from coming over right away, but he promised to be there just after lunch. She sat quietly, looking around her house. She thought about all the birthday parties, holiday gatherings and other good times she and Curtis had spent there together. Now that they were divorcing, the place didn't seem the same. There was a loneliness inside the home.

She thought about Nikki's upcoming graduation in May. She and Curtis were not the only people that would be moving on. Nikki would also be looking for a new place to come home to. Jess loved her daughter more than anything on earth. All the more reason to apologize and put things between them back on track as soon as possible. She called her to start that process immediately.

Rolly arrived later that afternoon. When she met him at the front door, she didn't offer the warm welcome that he had become accustomed to, she was rather standoffish. He figured she was still upset from what had occurred the day before. He spent a few minutes looking around her home. The pictures hanging on the walls were of great interest to him.

Rather than get cozy on the couch, Jess took a seat at the kitchen table. His instincts told him something was about to happen. She was acting strange. He didn't know what it was but was about to find out. He hung his hat on the back of the chair and sat down across the table from her. She didn't waste time with small talk. She started by saying, "Rolly I asked you to come here because I have something to tell you."

"Ok then, tell me…I'm listening."

"It's hard, you're going to hate me and I'm sorry." Their eyes were locked on each other. They just sat silently, staring at each other. In his gut he knew what she was about to say.

Finally, he told her, "Well, Jess, I can't read your mind so just say it."

"I'm seeing someone else."

Hearing those words stung him, but he kept his composure and asked, "How long have you been seeing him?"

"For a while."

He looked down at the table with his thoughts racing. Now it all made sense, the attachment to her phone, the constant texting, the sudden short unannounced trips out of town, and the little white lies. He knew now what had been going on, just not to what degree. He looked back up at her and said, "I have only two questions and I need the truth. That first time I met you at the truck stop…where were you coming from?"

"We were coming back from Fort Worth."

"Were you with this guy that day?"

"Yes, I was."

"Ok, the day you called me to go help Nikki with the flat…were you with him then?"

She shot back, "Where are you going with this? What does it matter?" She knew full well where he was going with his questions, and he was spot on.

"Tell me, were you with him then?"

"Yes, Rolly, I was."

"How could you do this to me, Jess?"

"Do what? What is it you think I've done? Let me remind you that I had a life before I met you. Let me also remind you that it was you that came beating on my door, remember?"

He retorted, "Well, you damn sure answered the knock without much work from me."

"That is complete bullshit."

He stood up from the table and said, "I gotta go, I need to think about all this."

Stubborn and defiant, she came back with, "That's fine, you go ahead and take your time and think about everything. I'll just wait here until you're ready to talk."

"What's there to talk about?"

He wanted to stay but didn't dare. He turned and walked to the front door. He felt like he had been ripped into two pieces. Half of him was hurt, half of him was pissed off. Standing at the front door, he thought of three more questions. He turned to her and asked, "How did you meet him?"

"He's a surgeon, I met him at a medical conference."

"What is his name?"

"His name is Michael."

"Do you love him?"

"Yes...I do."

"Then is it over? Are we done?"

"Rolly, please slow down, can we just talk?"

"Right now, I think I just need to be by myself." He walked out. As Rolly walked to his truck, there was a strange, cold pain at the bottom of his heart. It was a pain he had never felt before.

Winter gave way to warmer weather and longer days. The rolling hills around Big Spring were covered with bluebonnets and other springtime wildflowers. There were other changes going on, as well. Tonya had broken it off with Frank. She was never that serious about him anyway and the episode back in December was the final nail in the coffin. They lasted a few more months but now she had blown him off completely.

Back at school Nikki had come to grips with the fact that her parents were splitting up. She had to get used to her dad living in Lubbock, and she finally met Michael for the first time. Her and her mother were not quiet back on solid ground yet, but they were working on it. As for Jess, the three weeks since she had confessed the details of her other life to Rolly had been harder to deal with than she thought it would be. Although she was slowly trying to put distance between them, she still had tender feelings for Rolly. She missed the late-night texting sessions, the lunch dates, and their occasional road trips.

However, the difficulties dealing with her feelings about him were just a mild inconvenience compared to what he was going through. For Rolly, it was a crisis. He had been through all the stages of disbelief, denial, anger, rage, sadness and despair. Above all, his loneliness was back. He missed her like hell. She was all he could think about. He developed a severe case of separation anxiety. It affected everything in his life. He began making stupid rookie mistakes at work and at the ranch. It wasn't long before others began to notice the change in him.

After a business meeting in Odessa, Hoss gave Rolly, who was at the ranch a call, "Hey, Rolly are ya busy?"

"Not really, I just finished changing the oil in the Dodge and I'm about to go start filling deer feeders with corn."

"Ok well hey, when I get to the ranch let's you and me take a ride to the back and check fences. I'm afraid that high wind last night might have put down some trees back there."

"Hoss, you don't have to ride all the way to the back. I'll go check 'em."

"Awww well, I haven't been on top of Blue in six months. He needs a stretch."

"Alright then, you're the boss. I'll have the horses ready."

"I'll be there in an hour or so."

"That'll work, see ya in a bit."

Rolly finished up his chores then saddled up horses before returning to the guest house to pour two tall glasses of iced tea.

Right on time, Hoss pulled through the front gate. The two men quenched their thirst then rode off together. The hour-long trail ride to the north fence line gave them time to catch up on oil field gossip and discussion about ranch business. Rolly thought it peculiar that Hoss wanted to ride fence lines. He had never shown such an eagerness for saddle leather before. The pair of cowboys crossed several streams and navigated gullies as they made their way along the ranch boundary. Finally, they reached the Colorado River. All fences were in order.

Taking the lead, Hoss pointed at the top of a flat butte and said, "Let's go up there and have a look." Once on top, they stopped at the rim and sat quietly looking out over the river valley below. Hoss observed, "Pretty sight, ain't it?"

Rolly agreed, "Sure is, I never get tired of looking at it." Rolly could sense that Hoss wanted to say something. Never one to beat around the bush, he spoke up, "Hoss, is there something on your mind that you want to talk about?"

"Yeah, Son, there is. I wanna talk about you. You haven't been yourself lately, so I was wondering if there was something wrong."

Rolly just shrugged his shoulders and stared blankly at the ground in front of his horse. He knew now why Hoss had dragged him out in the middle of the sagebrush.

Hoss continued to pry for information, "Is there a problem between you and that woman you've been seeing? Is that what's got you down?"

"I'm not seeing her anymore."

"Hmmm...I see. Well, did she give up on it or was it you?"

"I guess it was her, but it wasn't ever going to work. I guess I knew it all along."

"Maybe ya'll just need some time."

"Yeah, maybe but Hoss, to be honest, I really had rather not talk about it."

"Ok then, Son, but if you change your mind I'm here to listen." After a moment of silence, Hoss spoke up again, "I'm going to tell you something and give you some advice if that's ok. Rolly, women are like tumbleweeds. They come and go with the wind. I think you should go find yourself another lady friend. The sooner you do, the sooner it's gonna stop hurting."

Rolly thought about his words of advice then looked right at the older man and said, "Hoss, you have become a good friend to me. You gave me a chance when no one else would. You trusted me when no one else did. I really appreciate everything you've given me. I want you to know that."

Hoss just chuckled and replied, "Nonsense boy, I didn't give you anything. You earned it." They spun the horses around and headed south. As they rode along, Hoss began to complain, "Let's hurry up and get on back, this shoulder's bothering me again."

Rolly wanted to know, "What's wrong with your shoulder?"

"I don't really know; it's been aching on and off and it's making my fingers tingle."

"Hoss, that don't sound good. You should go have a doctor take a look at you."

"Nah…I probably just pulled a muscle or something."

Rolly prodded him, "No, seriously, you need to go get that checked out. My grandfather started complaining about his arm hurting then two days later, he had his heart attack and died."

"Well, maybe you're right. If it keeps giving me problems, I may go on in to have it checked." They made it back to the headquarters just before dark. Maria had their dinner waiting on the table.

In the weeks that followed that afternoon, Rolly began to question everything that he had felt for Jess. Was he in love with her or just in love with the thought of being in love? He came to the realization that maybe he wanted to be loved by a woman so badly that he imagined Jess did love him. He wanted love desperately, but he had been looking in the wrong place. It's true, that old saying, "Sometimes a man can't see the forest for the trees."

There was a woman out there, and she was easily within his reach. Nevertheless, he kept pursuing Jess. Maybe it was just habit, but he hadn't given up on her yet. Jess proved to be the more emotionally mature of the two. She loved Rolly, but sometimes love just ain't enough. After disregarding his constant attempts to reach her, she called him one afternoon and asked him to meet her at their old meeting spot.

After arriving at the boat ramp, they both acted as if they were total strangers. The casual affection they had once shared seemed to be no longer an option. The tone started out as if this was a business meeting. In a very business-like manner, Jess began to explain, "Rolly, I can't do this anymore. I wasn't going to do this over the phone because you deserve better than that. I called you here so we could talk face to face. Rolly, I can't talk to you any longer. It gets us nowhere, it makes things harder, and it's not fair to Michael."

He answered, "Since when are we thinking about fairness?"

"Don't go there…I'm trying to be kind. I didn't come here to argue. We should have never done what we did, and I'll take all the blame, but it's over. I just don't want there to be hard feelings between us." She then turned her back to him, crossed her arms, and hung her head.

Rolly wanted to know, "That's it? Just like that huh…after everything we've done? It's all over?"

Talking over her shoulder, she said, "Michael asked me to move to Fort Worth to be with him."

He asked, "Are you going to do it?"

Turning back to him, she closed the distance between them. Now, in a much softer voice she said to him, "Rolly, I have enjoyed every second of our time together and I will never forget any of it." Staring straight into his eyes, she continued, "I'm doing you a favor. You think you want me right now but trust me you don't. There is someone else out there that will make you much happier than I ever could. You need to go find her and I'm just standing in your way."

Those words would turn out to be very prophetic. She leaned in, wrapped her arms around his sides and invited a kiss. He accepted her offer. After gently taking her face in his hands, they shared the most passionate kiss either had ever experienced. When it ended, she rested her forehead against his chin and said, "Rolly, please don't make this more difficult than it has to be." She then pushed away, turned, and walked to her car.

Just before she got inside, Rolly said his last goodbye to her, "I love you, Jess."

With tears in her eyes, she hesitated, then looked back at him. She obviously wanted to say something but didn't. She got in her car, started the engine and drove away. At that same moment, his pain returned. That aching, cold pain tugging at the bottom of his heart. It hurt. Crushed, Rolly climbed back in his truck and sat, looking out across the lake, deep in thought. Less than five minutes later, he received an unexpected text from Jess that said, "Rolly, I want you to remember something. No matter what you see or don't see, just remember I love you. No matter what you hear or don't hear, just remember I love you. Goodbye."

He sent her a reply text that went unanswered. He then read the text slowly several times. Rolly didn't understand the seemingly cryptic messages she was sending. Hear or don't hear? See or don't see? What does that mean? The first clue was the next day when she blocked him on Facebook and all other social media accounts. The next clue was when he discovered she had changed her phone number. And lastly, she deleted her e-mail account. That was it. Jess had made her decision. She chose comfort and security over love.

Did she love Michael? She loved him enough, but she left her real passion standing in a parking lot back in Howard County. Nevertheless, when it came to relationships, Jess was learning to treat each as a business venture. She wanted the maximum return for the least bit of investment. She chose the path of least resistance. She had the ability to be stone cold. She wanted a completely fresh start and didn't hesitate to cut the cord.

Emergency
Ambulance Only
RESERVED PARKING
RESERVED PARKING
VAN ACCESSIBLE

CHAPTER 15

ROLLY WOKE UP a little later than usual. The sun was beginning to shine through the crack in the curtains. As he lay there thinking and trying to organize his plans for the day, his mind began to slip over to thoughts about her. Quiet moments like these, when he was alone with his own brain, were becoming painful. To avoid the anxiety, he sprang out of bed and got dressed. The morning was crisp and clear. With a thin layer of frost coating everything. The horses in the corral playfully chased each other in circles.

Rolly climbed up in the seat of the old tractor and used it to load four round bales onto a flatbed trailer. He then hooked onto the trailer and drove through the front gate of the ranch to take fresh hay to the cattle pens on the opposite side of the ranch. When he arrived at the east barn, one of the cowboys was there waiting to unload the hay with another tractor. He stood by as, one by one, the bales of hay were unloaded and distributed amongst the hungry cattle. About that time, the wail of a siren could be heard up on the highway. Rolly looked up as an ambulance raced by, but he gave no thought to it. As the last bale came off the trailer, his cell phone rang. It was Maria.

"Rolly please come back! Something has happened." Listening to her panicked voice, he knew there was something terribly wrong.

"What happened, Maria? What's going on?"

"Hoss is sick, something is wrong with him. Please hurry!" He immediately ran to the trailer hitch and unhooked from the tailer, then left in a cloud of dust headed back to the ranch headquarters. He pushed his truck to its limits for four miles. When he reached the front gate, he encountered an ambulance coming out with its emergency lights activated. He pulled aside to let it pass. He was undecided what to do. Should he turn around and follow the ambulance, or check on Maria?

He continued on to the main ranch house and saw Maria and her young son sitting on the porch. Both were crying. When he got out of the truck, Maria ran to him and collapsed in his arms. Sobbing uncontrollably, she told him the terrible news. Maria explained that she had finished preparing breakfast and had set the table. Then, Hoss came down the hallway and sat down to eat. Suddenly, he dropped the glass he was drinking from and attempted to stand up. Instead, he collapsed on the floor. She dialed 911. Maria continued by saying, "They said his heart was bad."

"Could he speak, did he say anything?"

"No, no Rolly…his eyes were open but he did not say anything."

Under his breath he mumbled, "Well, fuck!"

Rolly hugged Maria and told her he would be back when he could. He jumped back in the truck and went to town. He rushed through the emergency room doors and went straight to the receptionist sitting behind the glass. Before the woman could ever say a word, Rolly looked past her and saw Jess standing at a counter shuffling papers on a clipboard. She looked up and saw him at about the same time. Jess leaned over the top of the counter and pushed a button that opened the double doors to the emergency room hallway. He quickly walked through the doors and they closed behind him. As he stood in front of her, there was an awful silence. Finally, he asked her, "Can you tell me anything?"

Jess just slowly shook her head from side to side. "He didn't make it. He's gone, Rolly." He dropped his head, closed his eyes, and rested his hands on his hips. Jess tried to console him. Wrapping her arms around him she said, "I know he meant a lot to you. I'm so sorry." She went on to explain that Hoss never really had a chance for resuscitation. "It was a massive heart attack and he was too far gone, long before arriving at the hospital."

A million thoughts were racing through his head. What now? What do I need to do? What's the next step? He had encountered a similar situation after the passing of his grandfather. Rolly was reminded of the turmoil and grief that he knew was coming now. He hugged Jess once more and said, "I need to go."

She again tried to comfort him. "I understand, if I can help, I'm here."

Word has a way of traveling fast in small Texas towns. When Rolly came back through the double doors, the waiting room was full of people, including all the cowboys from the ranch and Hoss' business partner. They all wanted to know the same thing but perhaps for different reasons. Rolly delivered the awful news. The cowboys were looking for guidance and hope. He gave them both. "Guys, nothing changes for now. Just keep doing what you've been doing. Do you all understand? Nothing changes."

As he promised her he would, he rushed back to the ranch to check on Maria. When he made it back to the main ranch house, Maria was sitting quietly on the couch with an envelope on her lap. He tried to be delicate but she already knew. She didn't cry. She had already shed all the tears she had to give. Maria held out the envelope and handed it to Rolly and said, "Hoss told me if anything ever happened to him, I was supposed to open this. Will you, please? I just can't do it."

He asked her to give him a few moments. Rolly went outside onto the front porch and sat down in the big wooden rocking chair that Hoss used to sit in each morning. Hoss didn't have much family, at least not nearby. His wife had run out on him years ago. He did have two adult daughters. Gail, who lived in Colorado with her husband, and Fiona, who lived in Florida. Rolly didn't know much about either one of them. He assumed whatever was in the envelope would concern them. He was about half right.

Upon opening the envelope, Rolly found it contained a typed letter with information about where to find his will. Also, it included several bank account numbers, the name and phone number of a prominent attorney in Midland and contact phone numbers for Gail and Fiona. At the bottom of the type-written page was a handwritten note that simply said, "Maria, thank you for all you have done for me. You are my family. I love you, Hoss." Rolly stood up and went back inside to give Maria the letter to read. Maria discovered she did have more tears to shed.

Rolly determined that, as ranch foreman and close friend, the burden of notifying Hoss' daughters fell upon him. He called Gail in Denver first. She sounded as if she felt the remorse that would be expected from a woman who had just been told she lost her father. The call to Fiona was a little different. When she picked up the phone Rolly asked, "Hello, can I speak to Fiona Spurling?"

"This is she, how can I help you?"

"Fiona, my name is Rolly Burnett. I'm calling you from Texas. Ma'am I'm afraid I have some bad news."

"Does this news concern Hoss?"

"Yes ma'am, it does."

"Yes, ok then go on."

'Well, there's no good way to tell you this so I'll just go ahead and say it. Your father passed away this morning. He died of a heart attack."

There was no sound on the other end of the call until she asked, "Who are you?"

"My name is…"

Cutting him off, "No, no, I don't need your name. What is your relationship to Hoss?"

"I'm his ranch foreman."

"Can you be reached at this number you are calling me from?"

"Yes, ma'am."

"Thank you for calling. I'll be back in touch with you later, I may have some questions."

"Yes ma'am that will be fine."

She hung up without another word.

Four days passed. Hoss, like a true businessman, was always looking ahead. He had pre-paid his funeral service and made all the arrangements. His funeral was well attended. Many folks from all over the big country came to pay their respects to the huge, jolly, kind-hearted man who had touched so many lives. The service was officiated by a local pastor. Rolly, Manny, and the four cowboys from the ranch served as pall bearers. Hoss was laid to rest near his boyhood home of Monahans, next to his parents. The old cowboy had spent most of his life poking holes in the West Texas dirt. Now, his work was finished.

CHAPTER 16

THE READING OF THE WILL occurred at the office of Hoss' personal attorney. That attorney had summoned all the parties with an interest or that had been mentioned in the document. Hoss named a rancher friend to be the executor of his will. Basically, Hoss' financial assets and all property were to be evenly divided between his daughters, Gail and her older sister, Fiona.

There were two notable exceptions. Hoss left Maria with a sizable amount of money. Then there was also a mysterious woman in attendance that no one knew anything about. Hoss had willed her fifty thousand dollars in cash. Obviously, there was some relationship there, but she wasn't talking. The very next day on the other side of town, lawyers representing investors, the two daughters, and Hoss' business partner, got busy drawing up papers in preparation to divide up the Spurling Energy Company and the ranch, like slices of pie.

It didn't take long for the winds of change to shift directions and start blowing through the lives of everyone who had worked so loyally at the ranch. Three weeks to be exact. While inspecting a job site one morning, Rolly got an unexpected call from Fiona. She asked him to notify all the employees of the ranch to gather at the main ranch house on Friday at five p.m. for a meeting. He agreed to deliver the message but wanted to know what the meeting was in regard to. She told him he would find out Friday with everyone else. He did as he was asked to do.

The cowboys all speculated on what was in store for them Friday afternoon. They could see the writing on the wall. Weldon, the most senior cowboy, told Rolly, "I don't like that damn Fiona. She reminds me of that green bitch that melted at the end of that movie."

Rolly almost busted a gut laughing and asked, "You mean the green witch in *The Wizard of Oz*?"

Weldon nodded, "Yeah, that one." Ever since they first met, Rolly was uneasy around Fiona. He didn't like the way she was always staring at him over the top of her glasses. He also did not appreciate the disrespect she showed her father by constantly referring to him by his first name.

When everyone began arriving on Friday afternoon, Fiona was sitting on the front porch along with Dolph Sinclair, the owner of Sinclair Beef based in Dalhart. His company was a remnant of the old X.I.T. ranch from the Republic of Texas days long, long ago. Maria was busy in the kitchen brewing iced tea and baking cookies. She was holding out hope this meeting would turn out to be positive.

Finally, everyone showed up and gathered around the front porch and the informal meeting began. Fiona got up and announced that the ranch was in the process of being sold to Mr. Sinclair. It was a process that would most likely take a year. In the meantime, Mr. Sinclair's outfit would be leasing the ranch. She went on to say that she would be living at the ranch full time until the sale of it was final. At that point, Fiona turned and walked into the house.

Sinclair took the reins then. He thanked the cowboys for their service, wished them well, and sent them away with an envelope that contained a final check and severance pay in the amount of three hundred dollars. One by one, the cowboys came by and shook Rolly's hand before climbing into their trucks and driving away. He was sick to his stomach. These were his friends and men he had built bonds with. Rolly could feel a bitter anger rising inside himself. He thought, "Yeah, it's now her ranch and she can do whatever she fucking wants to do with it, but this seems a little too coldblooded and inconsiderate."

After the other employees were gone, Sinclair addressed Maria who had been standing quietly and patiently to one side. He handed her an envelope just as he had the others and then said, "Maria, thank you for all your hard work. You will be missed around here, I'm sure. Your final pay is inside; however, severance pay was not included. I understand Hoss took care of that already."

Maria took the envelope then politely turned away and walked over to Rolly. Smiling, with trembling lips she said, "Please come by to visit me on occasion."

Rolly responded, "I will Maria...you know I will."

It took her a few minutes to gather her things and carry them to her little car. She crawled inside and drove away. Rolly was furious. As he walked up the steps, Mr. Sinclair was slapping his lips together saying, "Well, come on up young man, I've been wanting to meet you."

"Well, the introductions will have to wait just a goddamned minute."

Rolly walked right past him to the small table where Maria had set a pitcher of tea and a plate full of cookies that had not been touched. He grabbed the pitcher and poured it over the rail into the dirt. Then, he tossed the cookies out into the yard. Sinclair responded by asking, "What's all that about?" Rolly snapped back, "I wanted to make sure no asshole around here got to enjoy that woman's hard work."

"Is there going to be a problem?" Sinclair asked.

"Not one that you could handle, buddy."

The heated exchange between the two men was going downhill fast when Fiona re-emerged. "Rolly, Rolly calm down now. It's all just business. None of us is happy they had to be let go." She then asked Sinclair to leave her and Rolly alone. The old cattleman was more than happy to leave physically intact.

For the next ten minutes Fiona tried to sugarcoat everything, which was a ruse for what she was building up to. Then she delivered his fate. Rolly was to be relieved of his duties on the ranch but with a silver lining, if he wanted it. She offered to let him continue to stay at the guest house rent free. Being all alone on the ranch ten miles from town was not going to happen. She wanted a man on the place for security.

His instinctive reaction was to tell her hell no but then he thought of Jake. Leaving would cost him money that he had been funneling to his ex, Donna. Plus, Jake had gotten used to coming to the ranch on his short stays. He didn't want to jerk that rug out from under his son. He accepted Fiona's offer. Gail had turned over to her older sister the responsibility of selling off all their father's assets. Fiona was now in charge. She made the decisions now at the ranch.

Over the next several weeks, Rolly witnessed the sale of everything that wasn't tied down on the ranch. It was like buzzards on a rotting carcass. The cattle were the first things to go. Sinclair Beef replaced them with trailer loads of black cattle from Kansas. Then the trailers, tractors, and all other implements were sold off. Next, the saddles, tack equipment, and yes, Hoss' beloved horses. All of them were sold to the highest bidder. Fiona would have sold old Gus if she could have found a buyer. It was a shame to see Hoss' dream evaporate like rainwater on a hot rock.

As everything was being liquidated into cash, Rolly and Fiona had very little interaction. He wanted no part of any of it. For the most part, he was able to come and go without her getting into his business. However, that all changed one night as he was getting ready for bed.

Rolly was about to jump in the shower when he heard Gus growling out on the front porch. Looking through the front door glass, he could see the silhouette of a figure approaching from the main ranch house. He stepped outside to investigate. It turned out to be Fiona. She walked up the wooden steps wearing a long bathrobe and carrying a wine bottle in one hand and two long-stemmed glasses in the other. She showed no shyness by moving right up close into his personal space and saying, "We need to talk about some ranch business."

He smelled the alcohol on her breath and questioned her real motivations behind showing up on his doorstep after dark. Still, she was calling the shots around the ranch now and he didn't want to piss her off by asking her to come back in the morning. He stepped aside and pushed the door open for her. She slowly walked by while still making eye contact with him.

Once inside, she took a look around and observed, "Yes, I can tell a man lives here." Standing beside the kitchen counter she poured wine into two glasses and offered him one.

They returned to the living room where she took a seat on the sofa and he sat down in the recliner and asked, "Ok, so what ranch business do we need to discuss?"

She squinted her eyes, smiled, and said, "So business-like all the time. Why don't you just relax a little bit."

"Well, you said we needed to talk, so I just wondered what we needed to talk about."

"You, actually."

"What about me?"

"I've been wondering what your future might be here at the ranch."

He replied, "I was told Sinclair was buying this ranch."

Fiona suggested, "Yes, but not for a while. The right word from me might convince Sinclair to find you a really good spot." That angered Rolly. Whatever his future held, this woman wasn't going to have any say in the matter. He got up from the recliner and walked to the kitchen sink where he dumped the remaining wine from his glass. He thought about Hoss and Maria and all the cowboys. He decided right then he was tired of her shit. He turned back toward the living room, leaned back against the sink and just crossed his arms.

In the living room she had slipped off her sandals and curled up in the center of the couch. She patted the cushion in front of her and invited him to join her. "Why don't you come have a seat."

He refused saying, "I don't think so."

With a slight bit of irritation in her voice, she said, "Now, Rolly, if we are going to be living on this ranch together, we need to get to know one another better." He just stood silent, staring at her. She then took a last long drink from her wine glass and set it on the coffee table. Fiona stood up, slowly untied the front of the robe she was wearing, pushed it off both shoulders and let it fall to the floor. She was now fully nude as she made her way over to him with a wicked grin on her face. Pinned against the kitchen counter there was no way for him to retreat. She pushed her breasts against him and began to unbuckle his belt.

He grabbed her hands with a warning, "Don't do that."

She backed away with a scowl on her face now. "Are you queer or something?"

"No, I'm no queer, but I ain't that damned desperate, either."

Furious, she retrieved her robe and footwear. After getting dressed, she turned to him and hissed, "I want you off this property tomorrow. Do you understand?"

Rolly, with a smirk on his face, offered his reply, "Lady, there ain't a damn thing you've got that I want. Don't worry, I'll be gone."

He spent a couple hours that night packing up his personal belongings before trying to get some sleep. It was difficult. His mind was a jumbled mess, and it wouldn't slow down. He now had a new problem...where to live. Moreover, Rolly kept thinking about Jake and how he was going to explain to his son that the happiness that they shared at the ranch was now gone.

At sunrise, Rolly was on the move. Behind the big east barn sat his travel trailer. He hated even looking at it but it was to be his home once again. After hooking onto the trailer, he pulled it out near the front gate to check the tires and lights. After a thorough inspection, it appeared that it was road ready. He jumped in the cab and began to pull out of the front gate. He checked the rear-view mirror one last time. He saw something that made him bring the truck to a sudden stop. There was one last piece of business to tend to.

Rolly walked to the back of the trailer where a certain dog had been following closely. "Come on. I ain't leaving you here with this bitch, you're going with me." He picked up Gus and tossed him into the bed of the truck.

He pulled the trailer to town and set it up in an RV park that was under contract with his company. In just over a years' time, he had now come full circle right back to where he started. All alone living in a 24-foot trailer parked beside an interstate highway.

CHAPTER 17

ROLLY TRIED HIS BEST to put all the ranch stuff behind him and look at the bright side. He had lost some income but gained a lot of free time. He thought perhaps he could work a few more hours in the oil field and it would all be a wash. However, it was not to be so. One week later, the other shoe dropped. It was every bit as bad as the first. Early that morning when he rolled up into the parking lot in front of the maintenance shop, his field crews were all just standing around holding their hard hats. Rolly thought to himself, "Why in the hell haven't these guys left already?" He got out of the truck and sarcastically asked the large group of workers, "Did I miss something?"

Manny, who was making his way over to him replied, "Well yeah, actually you did." Rolly wanted to know, "What's going on?"

Manny went on to explain, "When we showed up this morning the yard was locked. Then, this dude showed up and told us to all go to the contractor's trailer. They let us all go, Rolly. They laid us off." By now, the whole group of oil field hands were standing in a circle around the man they had been answering to for over a year. They were looking to him for verification.

Puzzled, but confident that there was a reasonable explanation, Rolly said, "Guys I don't know anything about this but don't anyone leave just yet." He got back in the truck and drove around to the contractor's trailer. His stomach was tied up in knots. He was concerned for his men and their livelihoods, but he was just as concerned for his own financial well-being. He stopped short of praying but he whispered to himself, "Please don't let this be true."

When he entered the trailer there was Hoss' old business partner Lewis. Beside him sat his brother-in-law. Upon seeing Rolly walk through the door, Lewis snapped, "Glad you could make it. We expected you earlier." Pointing over to his kinfolk he then said, "Rolly, this is Glen."

"We've met before." Rolly answered as he reluctantly shook Glen's hand and then asked, "What's going on?"

Standing looking out a window with his back turned to him, Lewis, the fat, bald, wannabe businessman dropped a bomb. "Rolly, we're going through a merger and a down-sizing. Your crews don't exist any longer. The men have been advised already. They will still get paid through today and everything will be legal."

Rolly shot back, "What about me?"

'Well, that's what we need to talk about. Glen is in charge of operations now. He will explain everything. I've got to run; I have a meeting in Odessa." Avoiding any eye contact with Rolly, out the door Lewis went.

Now Rolly and Glen were alone. He didn't care much for Glen because their paths had crossed several times in the field and he regarded him as a brown nosing suck ass. At any rate, it was now Glen's turn to ruin his day.

"Hey, Rolly, I want you to know I hated to hear about Hoss." Rolly just acknowledged him with a quick up and down head nod. Glen continued, "Hoss said you were a good man."

Supremely confident, Rolly replied, "Yes, and I still am."

"Well. I would like to keep you on but all I can offer right now is a spot on a dozer or a frac truck."

"Are you fucking kidding me?"

"No Rolly, I'm afraid I'm not. I hate to say take it or leave it but…take it or leave it."

"What about all those other guys? Can't you find them something?"

"Sorry but no, the budget is tight, and we've got more help than we need."

Rolly's thoughts were darting around in his brain. He had a lot to say but needed time to think. He ended the conversation by stating, "I'll be here tomorrow but I'm taking the rest of the day off."

Rolly turned and stormed out of the trailer door as Glen shouted to him, "I need you here at seven o'clock!"

When Rolly returned to the maintenance yard, most of the guys had already left. The few that remained took the news in stride. This was the oil field, where it's easy come, easy go. Here today, gone tomorrow. They all knew the rules of the oil field jungle.

Manny hung around a little while longer before trading a handshake with his friend then driving away. Rolly just stood alone in the gravel parking lot. With his eyes closed, he turned his face up toward the hot Texas sun. He felt a numbness as he breathed in deeply, trying to get control of his emotions. How could this be happening? He felt as though his life were unravelling.

He drove back to his trailer and collapsed across his bed. The pressure he was under now was almost unbearable. All his plans had quickly fallen apart over the past month. It was now time to come up with a new plan, fast. He was totally sick to his stomach, thinking about starting all over again, near the bottom. He'd had enough of the same old thing over and over. After pondering his situation for over an hour, he decided that he needed to prioritize everything in his life, from least important to most important. With those thoughts there she was again. Jess was physically gone, no doubt about that. However, she still occupied space inside his head. He was more than ready to prioritize her right out of his life for good, but not before saying all the things to her that he never got to say. He wanted to say them to her face to face before totally letting go and moving on. He didn't want to have any regrets following him around for the rest of his life.

He grabbed his keys off the counter and headed for her house. When he turned onto her street, he could see her car wasn't sitting in the driveway as he had hoped. Maybe it was in the garage. He parked beside the curb and walked past the House For Sale sign, on his way to the front door, gathering his thoughts along the way. He would never get a chance to reveal any of them. Inside the house there was one person quietly working at a computer. It wasn't Jess…it was her daughter. He rang the doorbell. The person on the other side of the door could see him through the peephole. After jerking the door open, Nikki folded her arms across her chest and defiantly demanded, "What are you doing here?"

"Nikki, can I please speak to Jess?"

"What do you want?"

"I just want to speak to your mom, please…just for a minute…please."

Then Nikki launched into a blistering rebuke, "Haven't you done enough already? Why do you just keep hanging around? Can't you see that we're all trying to get on with our lives? We just want to forget you ever existed. Everyone was right about you. Mom is not here so please just go away."

He felt the air leave his lungs. His heart was in the pit of his stomach. Never before had spoken words hurt him so deeply. The anger and hatred displayed on her face was more than he could handle. He simply said, "I'm sorry." Rolly slowly turned away and walked back to his truck. The sound of the front door slamming was his only sendoff. He was numb with raw emotions as he inserted the key and started the engine.

Inside the house, Nikki was going through her own emotional rollercoaster. She quickly realized that she had just practically spit in the face of another human that she still quietly had feelings for. Her back was against the front door as tears formed in her eyes. A voice inside her head was pleading, "You are not this cruel, this is not you. Don't do this." Her emotions took control of her. She opened the front door and ran out onto the front lawn, waving her arms.

Rolly, who had now turned around in the cul-de-sac, was headed in the opposite direction. Upon seeing her, he stopped in the middle of the street. She walked in front of his truck around to the passenger side. She opened the door and crawled up into the cab with him. Both of them just sat in silence, looking out the front windshield. Finally, Rolly asked, "Did you think of a few more insults that you forgot to hurl my way?" Snot and tears, along with her makeup, were flowing down her face.

"Rolly, I'm sorry. I'm so sorry I said those things. Please forgive me, I didn't mean any of it."

"Ok, I forgive you, what now?"

"I don't know, things are just so fucked up."

"Yeah, tell me about it."

"Rolly, a lot of shit has happened and I don't know how to deal with any of it. I guess you came here wanting to talk. Well, I would really like someone to talk to also. If you want to talk about it all, then so do I."

"Nikki, is your mom really gone?"

"Yes, she's with Michael in Fort Worth."

He took a deep breath, shifted into drive, and just started driving. They ended up at the spot all too familiar to him, the boat ramp parking lot again. Rolly and Nikki sat for two hours as he told her about the details of his relationship with her mother, from start to finish. She then gave him the story from her perspective. After they had both said their piece, he told her, "I'm really sorry, the whole thing was one big mistake. It should have never happened, it just did."

Nikki then offered her own apology. "Rolly, I'm sorry about what I did in San Angelo."

He answered, "Are you kidding me? Hell, I had that coming. I'm just glad you'll still talk to me."

From that moment, the conversation took a lighter tone. They even shared a few laughs. When it was over and time to leave, they both felt better. He no longer felt the need to say anything more to Jess. He just had his opportunity to say everything he needed to say. Nikki finally got a lot of things off her chest, as well.

Just as they were about to leave the boat ramp parking lot, a green pickup truck with an official looking emblem on both doors and pulling a boat drove in. Nikki asked, "Who is that?"

Rolly told her, "That's the game warden." As the truck passed by, the officer inside offered a small wave. Rolly commented, "I always thought that would be a really neat job to have." They left the parking lot and he dropped her off at her house with the promise to call if he still needed to talk.

When the sun came up the next morning, he was at the maintenance yard. There, he had his company truck taken from him, he was assigned to a bulldozer, and advised of his reduction in pay. He spent the next eight hours digging an overflow pit. It was hard, hot, dirty work. Those things he didn't mind, he wasn't afraid to work. The problem was the work was demeaning. A man with his experience and skill set had no business digging holes.

At the end of the workday a co-worker dropped him off at his trailer shortly before six o'clock. He was met at the door by a furry friend. After letting Gus out for a short walk, Rolly let him back inside. Rolly drank a glass of water at the kitchen sink before going to the restroom to get out of his filthy clothes. After getting undressed, he stood in front of the mirror staring at himself. He didn't recognize the person looking back at him. He looked tired and beaten. The small wrinkles around his eyes were new to him. The lines across his forehead were more pronounced than ever. The dark bags underneath his eyes shocked him into reality.

It was time to sink or swim. It was time to pick up the broken pieces and put his life back together. After washing the dirt off his face, he turned away from the mirror and began the long walk through the rest of his life. It had been one year, four months, thirteen days and ten hours since he laid eyes on Jess for the first time. In that time, he chased her, caught her, built a relationship, and fell in love with her…or did he? It didn't matter any longer, he was done. That was all over now. In that same time, he'd also gone from nothing and began to rise to the top, only to be pushed back down again. He committed himself to never repeating that cycle. He had come up with a plan and was going to pursue that plan with every ounce of energy he had.

CHAPTER 18

NIKKI DIDN'T LET the upheaval between her parents affect her own life. She got busy preparing for her own future. The internship at the clinic in Midland turned into a full-time position. She also began working toward a master's degree at the university in Odessa, just down the road. Rolly and Nikki stayed in touch and began to form a close friendship. They were not officially dating, but their casual relationship began to move in that direction.

After not hearing from her for over a week, Rolly was surprised one afternoon to arrive at the trailer to find Nikki sitting on the hood of her car waiting for him. Stepping out of his truck, he asked, "What brings you here?"

"I brought pizza, are you hungry?"

"Well, yeah but how did you know I would be here?"

"I figured you would be here. What else do you have to do after work besides eat pizza with me?"

He laughed and put his hat on her head. Inside the trailer Rolly, Nikki, and Gus were eating cold pizza when she told him, "Hey, momma finally sold the house so I gotta move out."

"Where are you going? What are you gonna do?"

"I'm moving into a rent house that belongs to a friend of my mom."

Rolly was curious, "What friend?"

"Her name is Tonya."

"Oh, Tonya, that figures."

"Do you know her?"

"Yeah, we've met. She's a real peach."

"Hey, Tonya's a little different I admit, but she's always been really good to me."

"Why did you even come back here? Your parents aren't even here now."

Nikki shrugged her shoulders and said, "It's home to me. It's all I've ever known."

He observed, "But you don't have any family here. I wonder why they didn't have any more kids."

"I was supposed to have a brother."

He stopped, looked at her and asked, "What do you mean?"

"Momma lost the baby. She never told you that?"

"No, she didn't."

"I don't remember much about that except Momma cried a lot." Rolly quietly ate his pepperoni, thinking about Jess. He realized there was probably a whole lot she never told him. He then shifted the conversation back to Nikki. He had a specific topic in mind he wanted to discuss. "Are you seeing anybody?"

"No, not currently."

He pressed again, "No one, not at all?"

"No…no one."

"Have you ever gone out with anybody else more than once?"

Guardedly she said, "I've made a few mistakes."

"In what way?"

"Every guy I've ever dated turned out to be a big mistake."

"Oh yeah? Tell me why."

"They were all too immature and it's just this place."

"What's wrong with this place?"

"I'm just not into this whole cowboy thing. It's 2016, for God's sake. Time to catch up to the modern world."

He countered her complaint by saying, "Well, if you ask me, the modern world could use a little more of the cowboy thing."

"Yeah, well maybe. I know I won't be here forever but for now it is what it is." Then Nikki turned the tables asking, "What about you? Have you started seeing anyone else right now?"

"No"

"No one at all?"

"No...I don't have time for anyone right now."

With her eyes trained on him, wondering what his response would be, she asked, "Rolly, would you make time for me?"

He leaned back on the sofa and glanced up at the ceiling. He took a deep breath and answered, "Nikki, how would you ever be able to get past what went on between your mom and me? We were more than just pen pals."

She closed her eyes and covered her ears with her hands while tapping both feet on the floor. "I don't want to hear that." The room fell quiet. After a few seconds of fidgeting by both of them she spoke up, "Rolly, do you believe in destiny?" He just shrugged his shoulders. She continued by saying, "Maybe all this had to happen. If you had never met my mom, I would have never met you, and I wouldn't be sitting here right now. That's the way I've decided to look at it."

Rolly looked down from the ceiling and stared into her eyes. Then, he leaned forward and kissed her, but took it no further. The physical attraction between them was there. It had always been there. For now, they were cautious. They were taking it slow.

Game Warden
← Training Center

CHAPTER 19

SMOKE BELCHED FROM THE STACK of the bulldozer as Rolly began clearing brush and pushing up dirt for a road. The gravel trucks were scheduled to arrive first thing the next morning, so he needed to get the job finished. He was a little pissed that he had to work on a Sunday, but at least it wasn't the next Sunday. He had to pick up Jake then. He continued his work until noon when he then climbed down out of the cab in order to take a lunch break. As he was walking to his truck, his phone rang. He didn't recognize the number but answered anyway. It turned out to be someone he'd met before.

"Hello."

"Rolly, this is Tonya."

The hair on the back of his neck stood up as he replied, "Yeah, what do you need?"

"Rolly, I have something terrible to tell you. Jess has been in a really bad car wreck."

Her words stopped him in his tracks, "Is she all right? Where is she?"

"No, she's not alright. It's bad, Rolly, she was taken to the hospital in Fort Worth." Lots of things began rushing through his mind as he began to try to prioritize his questions. "How bad is it? Tell me what you know."

"That's all I know, but Rolly…Michael was killed in the accident."

"Does Nikki know all of this?"

"Yes, Nikki is the one who called me."

There was a brief moment of silence then Rolly put his feelings about her aside and said, "Tonya, thanks for calling me."

"Well. I thought you needed to know."

He ended the call quickly and began dialing Nikki's number. When she answered he could hear her sobbing. "Nikki, where are you?"

She cried into the phone, "Momma was in a car wreck."

"Yes, I know all about it but where are you now?"

Through her tears and pain she could barely get the words out. "I'm at my house but I'm about to leave and go to the hospital."

"Wait on me, Nikki. I'll pick you up and take you there. I'll be there in 15 minutes."

"Ok I will, but please hurry. I need to hurry."

"I'm coming, I'm on my way."

Rolly hung up and sprinted to his truck, then left in a cloud of red dust. Once on the highway he used his thumb to dial up another number. He wasn't looking forward to talking to the man on the other end of the call. "Hey Glen, listen, an emergency has come up and I'm going to have to take the rest of the day and maybe tomorrow off."

Glen demanded to know, "What emergency?"

"Glen I really don't have time to explain but I gotta go."

"The hell you will. I need that road finished today."

"I know but James or one of his guys is going to have to finish it."

"If you don't get your ass on that dozer you're fired!"

This was the moment Rolly had been waiting for. Glen had left the door now wide open for Rolly to say some things that had been on his mind for weeks now. "Hey, Glen, hold that phone in your hand real close to your ear. Do you got it there? Take that dozer and stick it up your ass…I quit."

He pitched his cell phone in the seat beside him and raced to pick up Nikki. When he pulled up in front of her little rent house, she was standing on the front porch talking on the phone. She was a pitiful sight. Tears were running down her face as she got an update from her grandmother in Fort Worth. Rolly leaned across the cab, pushed the passenger door open and shouted, "Come on, let's go!" She ran across the yard to his truck, carrying a leather bag stuffed with clothes. Not much was said between them until they got on the interstate. But then Rolly began to ask questions. "How bad is she hurt?"

"I don't know, Grandma just said she's in surgery and they won't let anyone in to see her."

"How did it happen? What caused the wreck?"

"All I know is her and Michael were going to see the Cowboy game. She texted me this morning and told me."

He looked over at Nikki and in a hushed voice said, "Tonya told me about Michael…I'm sorry."

She just covered her face with her hands and began to cry.

On the three-and-a-half-hour trip to Fort Worth, Rolly and Nikki would find out the horrible details of the car wreck through constant phone updates. They would learn that Jess and her soon to be husband were driving to the stadium to watch the Cowboys take on the Buccaneers in the NFL season opener. Somewhere along the way in Arlington, they were rear ended by a semi-truck. The impact caused their vehicle to flip over and slam into a concrete pillar under an overpass.

Michael was killed instantly. Jess sustained internal injuries, broken bones, and third degree burns over fifty percent of her body. The fire department had to tear the car apart to get her out. Doctors were now fighting to save her life.

When they arrived, hospital staff led them into the waiting room where Jess' mother, father, and older brother were anxiously awaiting any news from the surgery room just down the hallway. The grandparents hugged their granddaughter and tried to assure her that her mother was a fighter. She would be ok. Rolly sat quietly in a corner chair. He began to have feelings of guilt and questioned himself, "Should I even be here?" He was aware that everyone in the room, but Nikki was probably wondering who he was.

A couple of hours passed without any word. The growling in his stomach reminded Rolly that he hadn't had a thing to eat. He quietly slipped out of the room to go visit the vending machines in the cafeteria. After retrieving a packaged sandwich, he turned to see Jess's mother approaching him. She introduced herself and he did, likewise.

"Yes, I've heard your name, Jess spoke of you." Rolly was at a loss for words. He could not imagine what Jess could have told her mom about him, or why she would have talked to her about him. The encounter had him completely tongue-tied. She could see the uneasiness in his eyes. Mrs. McBride took his hand in hers and said, "I want to thank you for getting Nikki here. We were all very worried about her."

"Yes, ma'am so was I, that's why I brought her myself."

Still holding his hand, she moved in closer and said, "Young man, don't be troubled, everything is alright." She just smiled and walked away. Rolly sat in a window all alone and finished his make-shift dinner as he thought about her words. What did she know?

Finally, at 6:00 p.m. a surgeon came out and briefed the family. Her condition was still very critical. He explained that if Jess survived the next 24 hours, she might have a chance. The doctor, a hospital chaplain, and the family all gathered together to pray. A little later, Rolly pulled Nikki aside and asked her, "What are your plans?"

"Me and Grandma are staying here tonight. What about you?"

"I guess I'm going to get back."

"Grandma said you're welcome to use their guest bedroom if you want."

"Tell her thank you for me but I really need to get back. I kinda made a mess at work."

"Why? What happened?"

"I either got fired or quit. I don't know which one yet."

Nikki dropped her head and buried it in his chest, then wrapped her arms around him.

"Thank you for driving me here, Rolly."

"It was no problem. How are you? Really... are you going to be ok?"

"No, but what choice do I have?"

He pulled her tighter against him and rested his chin on her head. "I'll call you in the morning."

"No! Please call me when you get back to Big Spring. I want to know you made it home."

"Ok then, I will."

He pulled away and walked to the exit and out of the hospital. At the exit doors, Nikki never took her eyes off Rolly as she watched him make his way across the huge parking lot to his truck. On that terrible afternoon, a transformation was taking place. They were beginning to lean on each other. They were no longer simply casual friends. Rolly and Nikki had started building a tight bond. It was a bond they would need in the coming days. Sometime during that night, the unthinkable happened. Jess left her family and friends behind and departed from this world. Her body was just too badly broken.

Her funeral was held in her hometown of Stephenville at the family's church. Jess had a large extended family and a close circle of friends. They were all there. The former governor of Texas was also in attendance. He had been a freshman state senator along with Jess's father many years ago. He came to pay his respects to his old friend and colleague. The line of people waiting to get inside the chapel stretched out into the parking lot. Rolly stood alone beside the building. Numerous people noticed the tall, handsome, well dressed young man and went by to inquire about his connection. Rolly explained each time that he was simply a friend of the family. He waited outside during the service.

Inside, Nikki was heartbroken. She sat beside her father, trying to control her emotions, but that was impossible. The pain of losing her mother was almost too much to bear. At one point, Senator McBride whispered into his granddaughter's ear, "Nikki, your mother loved you very much. Life must go on. You can't allow this to destroy you or the life ahead of you. That would break your momma's heart." His words didn't do much to stop her pain, but it did stop the tears, at least for a while.

At the graveside, mounds upon mounds of beautiful flowers surrounded her casket. The preacher delivered some comforting words and then the family said goodbye to Jess for the last time. Nikki stood next to her father as the crowd began to slowly disperse. In the distance she saw Rolly walking away toward his truck. She let loose of her father's hand saying, "I'll be right back." She hurried to catch up with Rolly. "Hey, you.

You weren't going to leave without saying goodbye, were you?" He turned to find an obviously distressed but smiling young woman. Nikki hugged him and kissed the side of his face and said, "I didn't see you inside. I wondered where you were."

Rolly explained, "Yeah, there were not near enough seats, so I decided to let someone else sit down."

"I'm glad you came. I was afraid you wouldn't."

"Of course I was going to be here."

Nikki wanted to know, "Are you leaving now?"

"Yeah, I guess so…why? What are you about to do?"

"Well, I was thinking maybe I could catch a ride back with you if that's ok."

He agreed, "Sure, that's fine. Are you wanting to leave now?"

"Well, I'd like to talk to Dad a little bit and tell everyone else good-bye. My bags are at Grandma's house. Could we go by and pick them up?"

"Absolutely, Nikki, you do what you need to do."

The first two hours on the long trip back to Big Spring were quiet. The mood inside the cab was very somber. Rolly occasionally glanced over at Nikki only to see the back of her head. She intentionally sat turned away from him, staring out the passenger window in an attempt to hide her tears. She was still hurting.

When they reached Abilene, Rolly suggested stopping to eat. She agreed and they pulled into a small Mom and Pop café just off the interstate. They engaged in small talk over two chicken fried steak dinners. Getting some food in her stomach made Nikki feel much better. When they got back on the road, she was finally ready to talk. She recalled that Rolly had told her there might be a problem at his job. "Do you have to be at work tomorrow?"

"Uhhh…no, not tomorrow, not the next day, or the day after. I'm unemployed. What about you? Do you have to work tomorrow?"

"No, I'm off." She asked him, "So, Rolly, what are you going to do now?"

"Well, I'm not sure now. I was hoping to stay on with Spurling until I found out if my plans were going to work out or not."

"What plans?"

"I'm trying to get out of this stinking oil field for good."

She wanted to know, "How?"

"I applied to become a game warden."

"Game warden? You mean like one of those guys that checks your fishing license?"

Laughing, he said, "There's a lot more to it than that, but yeah one of those guys."

"Will you be the game warden in Big Spring?"

"Nope, probably not. If I get selected there's an eight-month academy I have to go to. After that, they can send me anywhere in Texas they need me."

"So, like, when will you know if you're in?"

"I've already passed an interview, which was the first step. Then, I had to go Austin and run, jump, swim and a bunch of other physical stuff. I passed that, too. The last I heard was I would get a call from someone who is going to do a background check on me. The next academy is supposed to start January 1st."

She noted, "Wow, that's not far off."

"I know. Anyway, until then I just need to find something to do."

Smiling, she said, "Game warden, huh? I like it, that fits you."

"Yeah, I really hope it works out. I'm sick of punching a clock. I'm sick of being filthy, plus I need something stable so I can try and get my son back."

Even though she was smiling on the outside, she was very tense on the inside over the news he had just broken to her. Was he about to leave? Was she about to lose her chance again? About that time, Nikki got a call from her grandmother. "Nikki, where are y'all?"

"We're in Abilene. We stopped to eat, what's up?"

"You need to watch the weather, it's getting bad out there."

"Okay, Grandma, we will. Thanks for calling."

After hanging up, Nikki pulled up the radar on her phone. "Oh wow, she wasn't kidding."

Rolly asked, "What's it look like?"

"Everything is red on the radar at home."

Rolly reached over and turned on the radio and tuned it into a local station just in time to hear an updated weather alert. The National Weather Service had just issued a Tornado Warning for persons living in Howard and Mitchell Counties. All persons were advised to seek shelter immediately. Doppler radar was indicating a large tornado on the ground five miles west of Big Spring, moving east at 40 miles per hour.

Over the next hour, Rolly and Nikki were amazed at the light show they witnessed on the horizon as they got closer to the storm. Twenty miles from home the wind picked up and pea-sized hail peppered the truck. The local news didn't paint a pretty picture of what was going on in Big Spring. Evidently, a tornado delivered a glancing blow to the south side of town. Power lines were down in some places causing widespread power outages.

By the time they rolled into town, the storm had passed on, but troubles had not. When Rolly turned onto the street to

Nikki's little rent house, it was blocked by fallen tree limbs and other debris as heavy rain was still falling. The only lights were the flashing lights from police, fire department, and utility trucks. Rolly told Nikki, "There's no use in you going home tonight. If your house is still standing, there's no electricity. Let's go check the trailer." Nikki was just silent and in disbelief.

They made a U-turn and drove to his trailer over on the east side of town. Fortunately, it was spared. The trailer didn't get a scratch and still had power. Rolly suggested staying there for the night. Nikki readily accepted his offer. Inside, she tried to calm Gus down as Rolly spent a few minutes trying to straighten the place up and make it presentable. Then he poured two glasses of tea and turned on the T.V. to get live coverage of the storm damage. Although it was bad, it could have been much worse. No one lost their life in the terrible storm that leveled a dozen homes on the edge of town.

When the reporters on the scene ended their updates, Rolly turned to Nikki to get her thoughts. He discovered that she was curled up and asleep on the small sofa. She was totally worn out. The past week had taken everything she had mentally, physically, and emotionally. He laid a blanket over her and let her sleep.

CHAPTER 20

OVER THE FALL, both Rolly and Nikki stayed busy. She put in a lot of hours at the clinic practicing her new trade and devoted most of her free time working toward her advanced degree. Rolly hustled around the oil field and used his contacts to find enough work to pay the bills while still chasing down his future plans. During Thanksgiving Nikki spent most of the holiday with her dad in Lubbock or in Fort Worth with her grandparents. It was the first holiday without Jess, and it was emotionally tough on the whole family.

With the exception of his weekends with Jake, Rolly spent his off time, including Thanksgiving, all alone. The past six months had been very difficult for him and as stressful as any other time in his life. But he was about to catch the big break he'd been hoping for. The first week of December he received an envelope containing a letter that would change his life completely. He got in! The letter advised him that he had been selected to attend the Texas Game Waden Training Academy. He was halfway through reading the letter when he said to himself, "Well, I'll be damned!" He couldn't believe it. He always knew it would be a long shot, especially considering there were over 2000 applicants for only forty positions. This was a game changer. The first step in his new plan had finally fallen into place. Rolly's first call was to his grandmother. His second was to his brother. Then, he called Nikki.

"Hey, baby girl, guess what?"

"What?"

"I did it…I got in."

"Got in what? Were you locked out?"

"No, you dope, the game warden academy. I got in."

"No damn way! Are you serious?"

"Yep…it starts January 1st…they told me to be there."

"Oh my God, I'm so happy for you! Are you excited?"

"I just got the letter this morning. It hasn't really sunk in yet, but we need to celebrate. Let me come pick you up this afternoon."

"I'll have to skip class tonight, but I guess I could."

"It's up to you but I'd like to take you out."

She excitedly agreed, "Yes, ok lets' do it."

That night he showed up with a Christmas gift for Nikki and over dinner, he explained to her all of his immediate plans. She listened intently to everything he had to say but she was distracted. She knew this all meant big changes were coming to his life. She just hoped that his plans might include a place for her. Even though she was very concerned, she put on her best happy face.

There was no time to waste. He had 23 days to get ready to report for the biggest challenge of his life. He began to get ready by paying off all the bills he could afford to pay off. Then he started gathering up all the equipment and supplies he had been instructed to bring with him to the academy. Along the way he worked a few odd one-day jobs just to keep some extra cash in his pocket. He quit the nine to five work altogether.

On Christmas Eve, he sold his trailer for cash. He didn't have much else to his name but what articles he did own, he put in a small storage room he had rented. The next stop was a trip over to his trusted friend's home. He was glad to see Manny had found new work and was doing well. He had a favor to ask of him as well. He told Manny about his appointment to the academy and explained his situation.

"Manny, I really need a huge favor."

"Just name it, dude."

"Well hold on. You better wait until you hear me out. Listen, I need to find a place for Gus until I get out in July. Is there any way possible you could keep him for me?"

"Yeah, that's cool. I've got this great big yard. That won't be a problem."

"Are you sure? I can't thank you enough if you can do that for me. I'll pay for his food."

Manny interrupted, "Don't worry about it. I'll take care of him."

Rolly unloaded Gus at his new temporary home.

"Good luck, Rolly. Give 'em hell down there."

"You can bet I will." The two friends laughed, shook hands, and then Rolly left.

The sun came up on Christmas morning to find him on his way to Sweetwater. He had called Donna the previous night and talked to her at length about his new career opportunity. He wanted to come by and see Jake before heading off to Austin, and he also had something he needed to give Donna. When he arrived, she allowed him to take his son for a milkshake.

During their short trip uptown, Rolly tried to explain to Jake about what was going on and what it meant for the future. Jake just smiled and giggled but he was too young to understand the implications of the undertaking his father was about to begin. On the way back to Donna's house, Jake opened several gift-wrapped toys and a new BB gun that his mom was certain not to approve of. When they got back, Rolly hugged Jake and wished him a Merry Christmas then told him, "I love you, son, now run inside and ask your momma to come to the door."

Jake pleaded, "What about my presents?"

"Don't you worry about that, I'll bring them. But, you go on in, it's too cold out here."

Jake disappeared behind the front door and soon Donna walked outside to meet Rolly. She asked, "When are you leaving?"

"I've gotta be in Austin on the 1st."

"Where are you staying until then?"

"I'm heading back to Big Spring. I've got a few other odds and ends to tie down before I leave."

Rolly then reached into his coat pocket and pulled out a large wad of one-hundred-dollar bills and handed it to her. It was all the proceeds from the sale of his travel trailer.

She asked, "What is this?"

"Merry Christmas. I hope y'all have a good one."

She just stood holding the cash and looking at him. She then spoke the words she had needed to say for a long time, "Rolly, I have made a lot of really bad decisions and there are so many things I wish I could go back and do over. I just hope you don't hate me. Please don't hold it against me."

"Donna, I don't. I just want you to take care of our son."

"You know I will."

"Then that's all I ask. Just take care of Jake, everything else is just water under the bridge."

A slight smile developed on Donna's face as she said, "I'm happy for you, Rolly. I can see you're going to make something of your life. I hope you make us all proud."

"I plan on it.'

As he walked away from the front porch, Jake stuck his head back out the front door and shouted, "Merry Christmas, Daddy!"

Rolly turned back, waved, and said, "See ya soon, Buddy." He returned to Big Spring where he spent the next six nights in a hotel room. It was the loneliest time of his life. He vowed to never let it happen again.

On New Year's Eve morning, he loaded all of his gear into his truck and drove to Nikki's house. When he stepped out onto the gravel driveway, he saw Nikki standing in the open doorway behind the screen door. When he walked up on the porch, she abruptly asked, "Who are you?"

Smiling and willing to play her silly game, he replied, "My name is Rolly Burnett, is the woman of the house at home?"

"I'm the woman of the house, what do you want?"

"Well, ma'am, I've got just the item every woman needs. I'd like to come in and demonstrate it if you would let me."

She couldn't help but laugh as she said, "Tell me more about this item, what is it?"

"A vacuum cleaner! Perhaps I could sell you one." He reached for the door handle and attempted to pull the screen door open, but she held it shut and barked, "Not yet! How do I know I can trust you?"

"You can't. I'm actually the big bad wolf and I've come to eat you. Now, let me in!" He jerked the door open and stepped inside the house as she stepped backward.

They shared a laugh before a more serious look came across her face. She knew why he had come by. This was the moment she had been dreading. Her stomach was in knots but she was trying not to appear upset as the only words she could come up with were, "What's up?"

"Well, I came to say goodbye. I've got to be in Austin tomorrow morning." Her nervous smile vanished as she turned and walked away to a back bedroom. He hesitated to follow her. He had wondered how she would deal with him leaving. He now had his answer. He walked to the end of the hallway and entered the room with his hat in his hand. He found her sitting on the edge of her bed crying as her body rocked back and forth. He stood hovering over her and asked, "What's wrong, Nikki? Why are you crying?"

With her voice cracking, filled with emotion, she replied, "I just feel like I'm losing you, just like I've lost everyone else."

He sat down on the bed beside her and put his arm around her shoulders. "Nikki, I'm not going away forever. This is just temporary."

"But I'm afraid."

"Afraid of what?"

"I'm afraid you're going to get out there and just forget about me. And then they will probably send you to God only knows where and I'll never see you again."

"Look at me." She wouldn't do it. She looked at the floor and just shook her head as if to say no. He demanded, "Nikki, look at me." This time she did look up at him through tear-soaked eyes. "I promise you will see me again, soon. I think I'll be able to come back on some weekends. We will get together as soon as I can, ok? I promise you. Now, come on and walk me to the truck. I gotta go. I can't be late."

She accepted his promise and the two embraced. She walked him out to the driveway where he left her with a kiss and a wave goodbye. And then he drove away.

Rolly arrived at the front gate of the academy fit for duty. He was grateful for the opportunity he'd been given. He looked at it as no less than his best and possibly last chance to get out of the oil field forever. The Texas Game Warden Academy was not going to be easy. It was one of the premier training centers in America with a reputation for turning out some of the best officers in all of law enforcement. It would require eight months of hard work and dedication to successfully make it to graduation. Rolly, having just recently reached his thirty-sixth birthday, was one of the older cadets. Most of the other trainees were in their mid-twenties. However, it wouldn't be long before his maturity level gained him the respect of all thirty-nine of his classmates.

Within the class, a tight circle of friends formed, with Rolly at the center. They began to look to him for guidance and advice. The instructors there also began to admire his preparedness and work ethic. In the classroom his test scores were always near the top. All the long physical hours of swim training, running, and gym work didn't seem to phase him. At the gun range he was a crack shot with both a pistol and a rifle. All his previous life experiences had prepared him well for this undertaking and it became obvious to everyone that Rolly Burnett had found his calling.

It wasn't until the last week of January that he got his first chance to get away from the academy for a weekend. On Friday afternoon, he headed back to Big Spring. He picked up Jake on the way, then checked into a nice hotel, where they got settled in. The next morning, he went looking for Nikki. She wasn't hard to find. The three of them spent most of Saturday in the hotel room eating tacos, watching T.V. and catching each other up on life's events.

Nikki and Jake were very interested in Rolly's stories about the academy. She had some good news of her own. Nikki had landed a new high paying job at a sports injury rehab clinic. The weekend passed by much too fast. But this became the routine for a while. Every second and fourth weekend when he could, Rolly gathered his son and Nikki together. It was during one of those weekends together that Jake did it again. At the city park, Rolly and Nikki were sitting on his tailgate talking as Jake played on a swing set nearby. All at once, Jake stopped and confronted Nikki with a question and a demand.

"Nikki, are you my daddy's girlfriend? I want you to be his girlfriend." Rolly recalled a very similar situation with Jess and held his breath, thinking, "Oh no, not that again."

Nikki thought about what Jake had asked and answered him, "I don't know Jake, maybe you should ask your daddy that question."

Jake's face lit up and he directed his attention at his father, "Daddy, is Nikki your girlfriend?"

Rolly breathed in deeply, looked over at Nikki, and smiled. They looked into each other's eyes and then came the moment she had been waiting for. Rolly looked back at Jake and boldly said, "Yep, Jake, I guess Nikki is my girlfriend."

Nikki leaned into him as she took his hand in hers. Rolly wrapped his arm around her neck and kissed the top of her head. Jake excitedly spun in a circle then began waving his arms and pumping his little fist up and down. Over the next several months it was moments like these that brought all three of them closer together.

Spring came and went. As the end of training at the academy began to get close, Rolly started to look beyond Austin, at what his future might hold. He thought about everything he had been through over the past two years, but spent more time now thinking about the next twenty-five years. He wondered where he would be stationed. He didn't have a clue but was determined to make the best of it regardless of where he ended up. He started to make other plans as well.

The last Friday in July finally arrived. It was graduation day. All the game warden cadets gathered together with their families and friends at the Texas State Capitol building in Austin to celebrate and receive their badges. Duty assignments for the new wardens had been passed out the previous week. Rolly's first field assignment was going to be on the Texas Gulf Coast along with his roommate, Danny Chavez. The graduation ceremony began at 3:00 p.m. sharp. Each cadet had been allotted five passes for the guests of their choice. Rolly would be accompanied by his older brother Walter, his young son Jake, his former in-laws, and of course, Nikki. His decision to invite his brother was a no-brainer. Walter was the closest relative he had that he cared about besides his elderly grandmother and son.

The idea of inviting his former mother and father-in-law served two purposes. First, he needed someone to get Jake to Austin on schedule and then back to Sweetwater. Although they were on better terms lately, he certainly didn't trust Donna to do it. Also, it was his way of demonstrating that he held no hard feelings toward them over his divorce from their daughter.

He was most proud and relieved when Nikki arrived.

All the invited guests sat above the chamber floor in the gallery. The commission chairman gave a speech that was followed by a few words form the major at the training academy. Then, one by one each cadet was called forward to have their badge pinned on them. As Rolly sat quietly waiting his turn, he had mixed emotions. He felt a great sense of pride but a great sense of relief also. It was as if the weight of the world had been lifted off his shoulders. He knew that over the past eight months he had achieved a great accomplishment that would bring stability to his life. However, he was also very nervous. Rolly had other plans for that special day. He just hoped everything went according to his plans. Then, his name was called.

"ROLAND JAMES BURNETT!"

He arose from his seat and walked to the podium where he was greeted by all the members of the commission. The major pinned on his badge, shook his hand then said, "Burnett, I want you to know that I'm proud of the job that you did at the academy. I have no doubt that you're going to be one hell of a warden."

"Thank you, sir. I appreciate that and I promise I won't disappoint you."

Rolly then turned and waved to his family in the gallery. Within minutes the ceremony had concluded, and everyone began to slowly exit the chambers. He met up with Nikki and the others in the huge rotunda. Smiling at her he asked, "Well, what do you think?"

She smiled back and said, "Wow, I see why women like a man in uniform."

"So, you like it?"

"Oh, heck yeah, you look sharp."

He said, "I hope you can get used to it."

Rolly leaned over and picked up Jake who had been impatiently jerking on his pants leg. He then took Nikki by the hand. "Hey, come outside, I need to talk to you."

At this point, she had a weird feeling...like a voice telling her something. She also noticed all the other brand-new game wardens were standing in a circle around her and Rolly. He led her out the big double doors onto the outside steps. Every new game warden followed them. She knew now that something was definitely up. "What's going on? Why are they all looking at me?"

Rolly then asked her, "Hey, have you ever been to Aransas Pass?"

She whispered, "No."

"Well, I wanna take you there but first I have an important question to ask you."

"Ok…ask me."

Rolly looked at Jake. "Do you have it, Jake?" With a grin as wide as Texas, Jake held out a mysterious box. He took the tiny box from his son and then looking deep into her blue eyes, asked, "Nikki…will you marry me and Jake?" Rolly held out the tiny box and offered it to her.

With her bottom lip quivering, Nikki took the box and opened it to find a beautiful diamond ring. She covered her mouth with one hand as she held the ring in the other. Her eyes darted back and forth between Rolly, Jake, and the line of new wardens. A quietness fell over the crowd that had gathered just before she let out a loud, "Yes…Yes…Yes!"

There was a thunderous cheer as thirty-nine cowboy hats flew high into the air. Nikki leaped skyward and locked her legs around his waist and her arms around his neck. Rolly now had an arm full of boy on one side and an arm full of woman on the other. At that very moment, Rolly had completely graduated from his prior existence and entered into an engagement with the rest of his life.

EPILOGUE

THAT AFTERNOON on the steps of the state capitol in Austin, Rolly Burnett finally found a tumbleweed that he could hang onto. Nikki Coleman latched onto a man who would eventually make all her dreams come true. They were married in a huge ceremony surrounded by friends and family. It was the beginning of a long and loving partnership that carried the couple through thick and thin...good times and bad. Rolly and his young wife followed their ambitions. After bouncing all around the state, they would finally settle in the Texas hill country near the town of Fredericksburg. He would become a widely known and very respected lawman. Nikki would accomplish her goals as well. For years, she would serve as the head athletic trainer at the university in San Marcos, before opening her own physical rehabilitation clinic. Little Jake would eventually be reunited with his father. From that point he would be raised by Rolly and Nikki, along with his twin sisters, Brittany and Brandy. All three children would later attend Texas A&M University in College Station and graduate with honors.

About the Author

BENNY RICHARDS was born and raised in Hunt County, Texas. A 1992 graduate of East Texas State University, he made his profession as a peace officer. After over 30 years in law enforcement, Benny retired and launched a second career as a writer. In addition to writing weekly columns in his local newspaper, he has published several other successful books based on his years as a Texas State Game Warden. Benny now makes his home near the small community of Campbell, Texas with his wife Kristi.

Other Books by Benny Richards

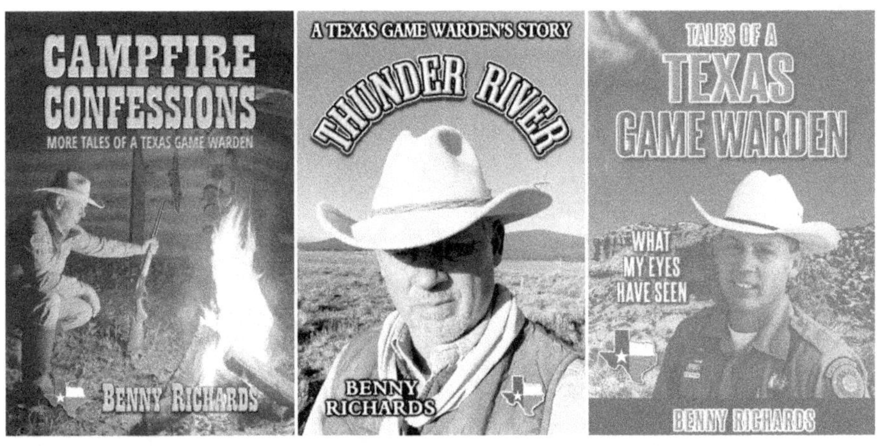